BIRDS ON A CAROUSEL

And here amongst us was an air that could indeed take the form of anything.

PASSIONFRUIT MARMALADE

There was a bright edge to the way I was speaking that night in Cobalt Market Hall. I noticed it the moment I told someone their bag was unzipped as they ambled by, unaware that a pair of vicious eyes not too far away was peering into the opportunity of a quick swindle. I was under the influence of red wine, but I realised I could be astute, if I wanted to be. I was standing opposite the little Korean karaoke bar, where jubilant mouths screamed that their hearts would go on, and on. A woman with vividly orange hair and lightning earrings turned to look at me. She was trying to light a cigarette with a matchstick and a steady concentration. The swishing fiery light I saw protruding from her eyes startled me. I wanted to tell her that I knew her somehow, even though I was sure this was the first time we had seen each other. She complimented my purple shoes, and as she did, I looked down at them; perhaps I wanted to remind myself of the way they looked, or I just wanted to divert my eyes from hers for a short moment. Purple. Purple shoes. It's funny, I had never actually thought about the fact that they were purple, a rich, vibrant purple that could not exist in a peripheral sight, a colour I'd never previously been drawn to until I purchased them from a shoe shop under the light of a lantern in Venice on a colourful whim. And now, as I looked at them, twiddling my toes underneath the fabric so it looked like there was a little creature at the end throbbing its tiny body to break free, I remembered a distinctly purple lighter I watched an old friend raise in the air as they threw their capricious urges around, enlightened by music; Roxy Music, it was, *More Than This*. Oh, how I loved that song. I remembered dancing to it with a bunch of strange faces at a disco a few years ago, and then I listened to it again, alone with my drumming thoughts and a little Tokyo subway map that I pinched at the centre and spun in my hand like helicopter propellors. Delightful memories. I quickly caught myself back to the purple shoes I had been staring at for ten, twenty, thirty seconds? Who knows. Oh, the vortex of wine. She was still looking at me, slightly perplexed, but at the tip of her gaze was an intrigue that reminded me of the time my old cat first saw my feather duster, which, like the shoes, I also bought on a whim.

"What size are you?" she asked, her eyes now fixed once more on my shoes.

"Eight," I replied, looking back down at them.

"I'm seven and a half. Can I try them on?"

She was brisk with her words; it seemed she was unthinkingly speaking, or speaking with as little thought as possible, and although astounded by her question, I admired that. So I nodded, removed them from my feet — suddenly feeling the coldness of the ground beneath the tattered layer of my socks — and handed them to her. Why was I being so trusting? I thought behind my somewhat congenial, somewhat disjointed gaze. I then watched as she took off her own shoes, placed them to the side, and then put on mine. Her feet slipped straight into them like moles into tunnels, and then, after a little hop and a skip, she dashed away, incredibly fast. As she ran it felt as though a thousand thoughts hit the forefront of my mind simultaneously. I stood there, stupefied and silent. Had I really just been so foolish to allow myself to be robbed? But then she stopped on the other side of the road, right where the pavement turned off to unseen possibilities, and she turned around, looked at me, and began laughing ferociously, her hands on her stomach and her whole body hunched over. And I, in my nervous consternation, began to laugh too. I wasn't sure if it was of the level of humour her laugh suggested, but as she laughed I couldn't help but join her in that zeal. Then she came back across the road, avoiding rapid bicycles and giggling gaily.

"I'm sorry, that was wrong of me," she said as she continued to laugh, "but I couldn't fight the urge."

"It's okay."

I knew I sounded puzzled, but there was a taste for humour in my words. I wanted her to know that I wasn't aggrieved at her little mischievous act, and although a little taken aback, now that she was back here and standing before me I could recognise the tickling hilarity in it. I could see that she was different, set apart from most people, that she was a wanderer, in mind and on foot, someone who meandered cheerily through the many passageways that life offers, the trails that many fail to see, and most who do see fear to wander down. And I was drawn to that, and then, within a burst of seconds, I found that we were both floating in some kind of kaleidoscopic bubble, together, surrounded by some invisible forcefield that held the spirit of mercurial thoughts within it.

"Look over there!" she exclaimed suddenly, her arm shooting up and her finger bursting swiftly out of her fist.

I turned my head to see people throwing darts in the corner of a bar through a window. And only a few minutes passed before we too were throwing darts in the corner of the bar, laughing together as we did. We were both humorously terrible at it, but it didn't matter to us. The pulses of our laughs echoed like sinuous sound waves curling out and up the walls, touching everything and everyone around, until we felt almost obligated to leave, to take our rhapsody somewhere else. Then we dashed along down the bending road, caught within the grasp of some kind of wilful ecstasy. Somehow our synchronised footsteps lead us to a pulsing nightclub, where bright colours flew themselves around in sparks on limbs that shot out from sweaty torsos, and smiles sent little glimmers of loose pleasure poking out of the dark and sweeping across the illuminated disco floor. We were glowing, wildly animated and present in the gazes of our sunny eyes. And her eyes, could they have shone any brighter? And my own, were they shining just as brightly as hers? Perhaps they were; perhaps our eyes danced like four little orbs of light, beaming and moving in bursts within dark shelter like fireflies alight in a cave. It felt as if our arms moved by the whims of their own minds, like we were the toys of giants, but unaware of it, unaware that we were puppets dangling from strings, forced to move by the control of much larger hands. But we were brilliant; we moved in a manner of unbridled light. And it wasn't very long until we felt the urge to move onto something new, to let the night carry us into its eddying swirls of potential.

Outside, I could feel the remnants of lingering bass frequencies thrumming through my eardrums, and I knew she could too, but the feeling was comforting in some bizarre way. Then I realised, briskly, that I didn't even know her name, nor she mine, in fact, during this time we had told each other not a single thing about ourselves; all we knew about one another was the sound of our laughter and the sway of our dancing bodies. I was hesitant to ask, partially because I found the unconventionality of this interaction amusing and I wanted to dive further into it, but also because her disinterest in telling me her name and finding out mine was fascinating. And I wondered how long we could go into this night together before she stopped to ask my name, how long it would be before she questioned who I was, and who she was to me, or if that would even happen at all.

As we walked, I couldn't stop myself from chuckling as I thought about the dreamlike events of this moment, the unexpected and fantastical happenings exposed to us from the corners of the unfolding night. Drinks and then laughter and loud music drumming into my spirit, followed by bright lights in flashing carousels of motion, caused me to become lost in a silent sandstorm of ideas and pulses of heartfelt emotion, a sudden taking of my being. Why was I having these feelings so intensely? It felt as though I had been uprooted from the only ground I was capable of understanding, and thrown into a new world where the language of the air was uncommon to me, an inauguration into a new season of myself. But, I quit my job that day, and the currents of red wine still swam through my veins, and now I was surfing the night with this orange-haired mystery, so perhaps it made some sense that I was experiencing this, this surge of unfamiliar movement, this electrical rush. I remembered my job — I had quit that very afternoon, and now it was all sinking in. I had walked out, in the midst of duties, duties so essential to me in the past that they had stuck to me like extra limbs. But today I had reached a limit of grievance, and so I left, and gushed out into the daylight with no plan for tomorrow. So how did I end up here? I thought for a second. Yes, that's right, I had taken my friends out, to drink, to celebrate, and after everyone had left, I returned to the market upon realising that I'd left my wallet in the bar, and immediately after getting it back, whilst I became swarmed with loud reverberation from karaoke speakers, we noticed one other, the two of us. And now, with our frenetic footsteps, we were approaching a bustling edge of the market, stacked with throngs and layers of sounds. Then we turned a sudden corner, and immediately we found ourselves dancing again. We danced into a room of other shadowy figures mingling and swooping around pool tables and televisions on walls flashing uncanny videos of speeding cars and jellyfish and spinning galaxies. We danced with bottles of berry cider in our hands, and moved a little too hard that we both spilled cider on the dirty artisan rug below our shuffling feet. Then, when we felt it was time to go, we threw ourselves back outside.

"I want to live forever in the refreshment of this air!" she called to the world with her arms out wide, connecting the stars as if she were embroidering the cloth of the sky.

I had never met anyone who used their words the way she did; in a way, she talked carelessly, but with so much precision. As I watched her praise the nature of this night, I was pinched all over by a sudden wonder: I began to think of time like a spiral, a spiral of changing particles through which we glide, a spiral with the weight of everything in the lightness of nothing. And for a transient minute, I was enraptured, sewn tightly into the fabric of pure elation. This vibrant spontaneity that had somehow swallowed me whole had taken me into a realm where everything seemed to be within reach, and I was ascending, sailing through vibrant impulses, open and ready for the surprise of every whirl and turn in our roads. And we were together, tethered to a great force that cloaked us in its canopy and protected us from the perils of the world, and we would go wherever the invisible nudge of this great force felt to push us. The night had wandered through us, soaked its hands through the seeds of our minds, and now we were growing with it, sprouting and blossoming like dandelions curving into the air.

Somehow we ended up coasting our way to a store in the corner of the market, a store with all kinds of colourful marmalade on display, neatly compacted in glass jars, with checkered lids and wrapped in threads that were looped in bows. Who would have thought that marmalade would be on display at such a time? We were drawn to the colours and the textures in the endless little walls of glass. With coins I found jingling in my jacket pocket, we purchased a tiny jar of passionfruit marmalade. It had winked at us from the shelf with its fantastical little pearls of colour. We sat down and she held it to my eyes so I could see it up close. I wanted to plunge into it, to bathe in its grandeur. The black seeds swam around in the lustrous texture of the distinct salamander-orange pulp; it was the colour of the most brilliant sunset, the colour of perfectly bloomed marigolds, of the monarch butterfly I had dreamed of in the recent summer. She fiddled through her bag and after shuffling her fingers through a myriad of things, she pulled out a miniature spoon. Why she had a spoon in her bag, I did not know. For moments such as this one, I supposed, for moments to capture the ever-giving sweet pleasure of taste. She then popped open the tiny lid, scooped a spoonful of the wonderful preserve, and shot it like a rocket between her lips. Only seconds later, my mouth was filled too with the sudden shock of sweetness, an intense pleasure. The flavour burst through like a flower from nourished soil. We looked at one another, our eyes opening and then closing as we became lost somewhere together, each of us becoming polyphonic components of such a vivid creation. And still, as we met on this plane of harmony, we were yet to find out each other's names, but as our mouths were caressed with such a divine sweetness, we were nameless. Or, in fact, we had names: she was Passionfruit, and I was Marmalade, or the other way around, it didn't matter. But that was all we were. Passionfruit Marmalade. And how distinctly wonderful it was to become enfolded by such a potently sweet, godly taste, together at the same time.

Where we would go next, I didn't know, and what would become of this interaction, I was unsure, but the night was still new, and so were we.

KERNEL OF BEAUTY

Here I stood, among the thousands upon thousands of solid structures, cascading to my eyes with their quick sharpness, their pristine edges, edifices and assemblies of mere convenience and lacklustre intentions. The greys, the silvers, the dark tones, the slender forms and pointy endings all around could not have pushed forth a greater distaste from my eyes. But still, I wandered through with a quiet hope to find treasure amongst all of these lifeless forms — perhaps an iota of patient design, a broken particle of something with a living essence. I roamed, each push of movement coming from some part of myself that wished only to find resonance, a connection, a physical manifestation akin to the home that lived within me, where I could blend into and become myself again and again. But in each sight, not a fraction came to me and befriended me; what was around appeared indifferent, almost hostile. It was a place where I could grasp onto singular components but not draw them into myself so as to call them friends of mine; they were strangers, strangers that only smiled and walked by, offering a minimal creak of interaction and then moving on, mindless of what I sought. I watched the world change from light to dark, and when the skies were unlit, I looked at this shadowy world of thoughtless forms, a world evolving with material objects and pieces of concrete and stainless steel, reciprocal with the character of raucous vehicles rather than the ones who move them. The silhouettes and clusters of identical shapes were prominent on the horizon. Below, the ground was lifeless, grassless, bereft of the breath of a respiring world. Above, towering industrial structures stole the kiss of the sky from the dwindling trees. If I squinted my eyes and focussed with a hopeful sight, I could find familiar faces within the shapes curtained around me, small features with some craft in their embodiment, but none of them approached me with enough to envelop me and fulfil me with the comfort I craved. Refractions, slick arrangements, glare and shine of polished glass, metallic structures. I couldn't stop myself from noticing the overwhelming uniformity, the lack of novelty, the shiftless repetition, the fear of colour. It was everywhere, and as my eyes glided through the corners of every crack, roaming the heaps and layers to find fragments of hidden curiosity, I failed to settle myself enough to be carried into a space where I could continue to be. I realised that I could not, even if I felt inspired enough to try, make this place mine.

But, below my eyes, I held a beaming torch that rose above the crux of my intentions, that whispered life into what it saw. And beneath it, my hands — with palms and fingers with a hunger to mould, to build, to craft a place that would reflect the source of my belonging, of my root, and of the root of others like me — pulsed and wavered, seeking eagerly to morph the world into what they knew to be true. Here, I was enveloped in a manifestation so distant from where I had come from, but within it, perhaps I could build a place for myself, a place grown from a kernel of beauty, constructed from the foundations of a home within me, a home that would rebuild itself, again and again, wherever I would step foot.

So, I began with a patch of land, a garden that would soon sprout from beneath my feet into the air, pulsing and shooting out lavishly all the wonders from the core of my thoughts, every detail and glaze and texture that somehow, if I aimed my intent in the right direction, could push out through the stratosphere of my vision and into tangible solidity. I sowed the grass seeds on the soft ground, scattering them and watching them fall into the soil, appearing before me like distant stars descending into the ether. I allowed the organic elements and unending mutability of nature to sprout these seeds into tiny seedlings, and witnessed them grow into thick strands of the greenest grass, beautiful and indivisible. When the season allowed me, I dug little holes into my healthy soil and planted flowers that grew up to my ankles. Rose, petunia, hollyhock, verbena; white, purple, orange, red, blue — they soon arrived in full bloom, ornamenting my blank canvas with the intricate colours of our world, here for me to behold evermore. I planted a tree and watched it grow to be a monument, adorned with the power of a deity, and the gentleness of spring's blossom. Its trunk stood firmly planted into the ground, secure, huge, sturdy like the foot of an elephant, and the many branches and twigs twirled and spread out vastly, tenderly grasping onto the wisps of the wind. This tree, so great and indescribably present, grew and fell into the sky the same way its heart fell into me in every moment I stopped to admire it. It enhanced the atmosphere and cast an unmovable beauty in the middle of such a cold bleakness, until the air found an essence to hold onto so it could become new and refined. And soon I was called to walls, walls that would shroud me from disconnection, walls that would encompass an abode full of unspoken dreams; so I built them around me on a portion of land shaded by the great hands of the tree, and above me I assembled a ceiling to cover me and catch the rain for me so I could thrill at the refreshment of stepping out to feel it. And I threw colour onto these walls, splattering every inch with crimson and cream and the abundant green of a godly forest. Along my thoughtfully crafted walls and windows, I allowed leaves to trail in any direction they pleased. Within these walls, what soon came was a world of great colour, and scents that made the nose wander, and paint and carved woods of oak and pine, and music, and glowing lights that emulated the sunset at its finest hour, warm and lambent on my retinas. I allowed songs to spring on the walls, and it wasn't long before the melodies escaped through the glass of the windows and called birds to warble into the chorus. And these birds found a home in the tree, a home from which they could sing freely and proudly, no longer cloistered in a world where they only knew estrangement. And at every dawn they began and would continue for every dawn to come, radiating the art that they knew instinctively.

Here I stood, nestled in a new creation of many more that grew out of a composed care, that flourished from the seed of a persistent forethought to yield a gift, a gift of enchantment, a gift that would keep on growing with me, and after me, moulding and carving and portraying itself in a habitual cycle. And here, in this new home, I could finally be.

TENDING TO A POTION

The unfurling blaze of the fire here moves fiercely. I can hear the crackling of the burning wood and it takes me away from the surface, where I've been all day. As I lean into the upholstery behind me, taken in persuasively and coaxed into winding down, the blinking flames catch my attention with the directness of a single emission of light, so acute, so compelling, emerging from the air with the bounce of a spring, the point of a needle. What is this familiar melody that sings? I know it distinctly; the memory of it is neatly folded in a hidden place deep inside the small but hollow space of my ear, and now I am being reminded of it again. Chopin, how could I forget your song? This haunting sonata has come back to me, after so long. I wander freely into the intermingling notes, reacquainting myself with the sombre but hopeful tone. Engulf me, sonata, show me your rising sun by raising me to the point of its sound, carry me with you. I close my eyes and see spectrums of patterns forming over and around one another, a superimposition of startling guests of luminosity. I am awake but I feel that I'm perpetually dreaming into something, sedating myself into the voice of the earth and then flying on the backs of winged beings that take me to a distant but familiar affection, a somewhat conjuring of hidden feelings. I'm wired into a beguiling journey, I'm traversing through tunnels of past and future memories, I'm being elevated into skies of infinity. But soon, time returns and the sonata ends, and when I open my eyes I see the fire again, and I adjust to the sway of its blaze as though I've returned from a journey and I'm settling down once more. My eyes water but tears do not fall, and I think this is because I wish to save them, for I suspect the music of tonight will outlive even this blaze. A new song has begun now, and somehow I feel as though it is speaking for us all, with its flares and its pulses and the story it so effortlessly summons. This particular nocturne is quite special to me. I remember the first time I heard it. It was many years ago. I had been walking through the trail of a lantern-lit pathway in the middle of a forest and a town subdued by the developing night. I was trying to find my way back to the hotel. The night was reaching a peak of darkness and I was beginning to worry that I was lost, but then I heard the faded edges of this nocturne, from afar. It called me, I listened, it called me again. Magnetised and convinced of a dream, I began to follow the route of the thread it laid out for me. I wanted to be closer to it. I couldn't remember the last time I had heard such a beautiful song, a time I had found myself so enveloped in the spell of dancing sound. My footsteps led me to a tavern enclosed by trees of night, with wide-open windows through which the reverberating notes soured. I stood by the windows, my chin up and my eyes closed, and before I could realise it I had melted into the song, like sleet melting into grass, the trickling wetness of it bleeding into the pores of sod, down into rumbling mud. I was caressed, stroked by garments of a tender nature, nurtured by a flare that lingers in the unseen. And in the music, I noticed a journey, the particular journey of this particular song, the reciprocal conversation that was growing and then falling and then inquiring and then discovering, swimming into questions and responses that begged new questions in a to and fro motion. And soon after, I stepped into the tavern, for how could I not? Inside, I noticed someone in a navy cloak sitting at an upright piano, whilst others around watched them play. I stood close by. I couldn't resist the desire to see the whirling fingers that moved along the keys, releasing such potency into this far-out world. How could only ten fingers, restricted by human limits, play with such divinity? I wondered. But these were not regular fingers, no, these were the filaments of an ethereal being; and perhaps I was the only one in the room thinking such things, but as the music grew and grew I was sure that all of us spectators had been struck by a similar amazement, that together we had touched the very tip of the boundary that borders the realm of which we have little understanding. Somehow I was made whole by frequency, pulled by unrelenting currents and introduced to a whole new plane of experiencing things, where curiosity flowed as naturally as running water, and awe came as easily as an exhale. And this pianist, they played like a wizard, and I couldn't see their face but somehow I knew their eyes were closed. They had sunk into the unfolding orbit of pureness in sound, translating it from its otherworldly form into an earthly movement, engraving it into the wind that came here to be a part of it through the open windows. Their body swayed, undulating in rhythms, as if they held a cauldron to their chest and inside it they were tending to a potion, stirring it, letting it respire into life. My curiosity held me there, and I stayed until the fading end of the last song, after the majority of people had left. And when the last song had ended and the piano lid had been placed down, I couldn't stop myself from going up to the pianist, tears on the brims of my eyes, and telling them how beautiful they played, how invigorating it had been to hear it all. In the wise circles of those two jewels of eyes, I saw the radiance of a childlike smile, and I don't remember exactly how, but we began to converse about the songs they played. Somehow we ended up staying there for a while, warm beverages in our hands. We talked about music. They told me about some kind of unfathomable nature they had found in the motion of getting lost to the piano keys, and that they played in order to get closer to it. They told me they felt that no one truly knew them if they hadn't heard them play. I told them that until that day I hadn't had such a revelatory sonic experience before, that through their playing, somehow I became locked into a silent conversation, where I had no choice but to surrender to the interweaving threads of stories in perpetual motion — stories after stories after stories, brought to life again and again through each push of motion. They told me that the more they played, the more they knew it but the less they understood it, that inscrutable element that binds a song. I told them I wanted to keep on discovering that thing I had felt when I heard them play, that spark, that bond between melody and the invisible components of how we perceive it. On a piece of paper, they wrote down a list from the top of their head, an array of songs they wanted me to listen to. I folded it neatly and held it firmly in my hand, and after saying goodbye, my footsteps keenly took me straight back to the hotel. Somehow I remembered the way back instantaneously upon stepping outside. And there, I sat at the edge of the bed, my arms resting on the windowsill, and with an old set of headphones I listened to each song. That night, that fine night introduced me to a world I hadn't yet known but suddenly found myself absorbing with an echoic fervour that stunned me, and with this enlivened focus I could assimilate every second, every note and syllable. The piano and guitar of great composers, ambient electronic music from the depths of East Asia, classic Brazilian samba, the raw lyrical folk of the 1960s and 1970s, orchestral compositions of the romantic period — I heard all of this, and so much more, one after the next, playing into me and out into the air with the vehement burst in the jump of a bird right before it sets off to fly. Before that night, I hadn't ever given a song the ears of my entire attention, and now I was feeling, not only hearing, but *feeling* through what I heard, every layer finely tuned to the circumference of me. Outside the window, through the pinpricks of rain drizzling along the vista, the world had never appeared so alluring; it was alive, and I imagined it breathing, unhampered by physicality, adorned by some kind of angelic flare from creatures beyond our sight as their travelling forms brush past our world of stringent outlines. I remained there for a long time, sedated, vapour rising from sencha between my hands, allowing the pulsations to merge with my thoughts, and my memories.

And now, when I open my eyes, I feel this new song with a sharp familiarity. This song draws a world that seems as though it's continually searching with the fine tips of many branches, finding parallels that speak to its core. I close my eyes again and allow the song to arrive, gradually, persuasively. Within it, I imagine columns of formulaic pieces piling on top of one another, moving elements infinitely on the brink of combustion, piercing tendrils in meteoric motion, a resurfacing of that familiar unknown.

And, after all, the music did indeed outlive the fire, and now, as the last flame holds onto to its few seconds of life, I fall into a sleep where melting hymns caress my eyelids and sew them tightly into the safe darkness of rest.

THE PEAR TREE

Someone once told me that if you are open to the many details of a day, a seemingly insignificant little facet of a moment can change your horizon of events. A symbol above your eyes, a smiling interaction, small passing words of a stranger — each day is full of these ephemeral fragments, throwing tiny signs in our direction, easy to miss if one moves mindlessly with their eyes on the ground, but radiant and multilayered to an eye that notices the quick-moving, minute patterns of a day laid down before them.

Today, on the rainy street of a block down the road from Avenue Montaigne, I had an encounter, a significant one. But for you to understand the significance of it, I must tell you a story, a story that trails backwards twenty years, to the wonderful, sun-kissed land of Provence, where I, a bright, hopeful child of just eleven, kissed the ground with my feet as I ran nimbly through the blossoming lavender to the bike shelter. Every other late afternoon, after I had crossed off the list of duties on the farm, I'd cycle down to town to pick up bread and raspberry jam and fresh juice or lemonade, and then I'd make my way down to the pear tree, and there I would eat and drink, leaning up on the trunk, with a book in my hand, usually one from my collection of adventure tales. I revered the stories inside of those timeless pages; I'd often sit reading for hours, unaware of nightfall verging on the sky. But my parents never let me out at dark, so when I'd notice the first slight squint of my wandering eyes I'd pack up and head back home. But on one day in the midst of autumn's fine burgeoning, after the harvesting of corn, wheat and barley, and I made my way with my book and a basket full of treats down to the pear tree, I spotted in the hazy distance a small, indistinct figure sitting in my spot. Fretfully, I hit the brakes and stood peering from afar. This person was young like me, that I could tell. I focussed my eyes as best as I could. It seemed to be a young boy, but his features were jagged and blurry in the distance and the blaze of the sun. I huffed as I stood and glared, my bike between my legs, my hand on my forehead to shade my distorted vision. This had been my spot, my own small nest in which I'd shelter myself alone with my adventure stories; in this spot I'd be rooted in the presence of my dreamful self, untouchable, left to my own volition, far enough from the rest of the world to find solace in peaceful solitude. That was until this moment. I thought about staying where I was and waiting for him to leave, or if I'd be able to conjure the courage to sit beside him and force him to leave with my striking silence. But then I noticed him lift something to his face, some sort of dark device, and as I watched his head move in all sorts of lines and circles I realised it was binoculars he was looking through, and now he was facing here, straight into my direction. Whilst a little stunned and aggrieved, I was glad that he was looking at me; I wanted him to see me, to know that he was intruding in my private haven, exclusively mine and only mine. But still, as countless seconds passed as our gazes clashed in the light of the lens, he did not move, nor show any signs that he was planning to. Conquered with some kind of brisk force, I put my feet on the peddles and cycled straight towards him. I thought I could scare him off a little with my tempestuous hurry, but as I drew closer, still, not an ounce of movement came from him. Instead, unmoving and resolute with a frozen spell, he just watched me through the binoculars. It seemed to me he was adamant about marking his presence, although thinking back now, he was probably ice-bound in fascination. In a sudden cut, I turned the handles and steered around, a mist of dirt scattering out from under the wheel. And then I cycled away, looking back with a stern stare before placing my eyes back on the road and speeding in the direction of home. When I arrived home I chucked all of my things on my bedroom floor and threw myself onto my bed, a rising rage of bitter fury pulsing through me. I lay there and wondered into the ceiling. I thought about the pear tree, how it had been my very own place of solitude and safety for years and years and how no one had bothered me there, not once. I didn't want to find a new tree, and I knew I wouldn't, so I convinced myself it was a singular occasion and he'd never show up again — but this hope was a fantasy. The next day, as the tree emerged invitingly on the horizon, I saw him there again. He was in the same spot, reading again, and upon noticing him from afar, this time something took over me: I began cycling straight towards the tree, determined to regain my spot. I wasn't going to give up this space that held the memories of so many tranquil moments. I just couldn't have that taken from me. As I approached, I did not permit my eyes to see him; I wanted him to think that I was unbothered by him, and I hoped that by inserting myself forcibly by the tree he would receive my invisible message and leave me to myself. I parked my bike, unpacked my basket and sat down, leaving just a small space between the two of us. A magpie, not too far away, came diving down and then swooped into a curve right in the air before us. The boy gasped in awe and then laughed aloud. His giggles, unapologetically careless and exuberant, displayed a strong sense of his restfulness, a demeanour in which he sat peacefully despite my presence, forcing onto me the certainty that he wasn't planning on leaving me alone. As he went on laughing I immediately felt a strong ambivalence: a tickling annoyance that he was still there, and a slight pleasant comfort I found in the hue of his laughter, as much as I tried not to let myself notice it. Somehow, though it was difficult to admit, his laugh sweetened the air between us. I reached into my bag to feel for my book, and as I did so I could sense him looking at me, waiting for me to give him a sign that I had acknowledged him. But I refused to let myself do that, my stubbornness wouldn't allow me, so I opened my book and pretended to read. After a minute or two, I allowed my eyes to steer off the page and turned my head just slightly, attempting to steal a devious glimpse of what he was doing. He too was reading, silent in his endeavour as an unheard breath of a tiny mouse. I studied him discreetly. He had on a worn-out plaid shirt with these scattered lines of threads all across, harshly faded jeans with grass stains that I supposed no one had ever bothered to scrub, and hanging from his belt were a handful of small bronze bells that trailed along in a playful row; one, two, three, four, five, I counted — this was strange to me, but I was overcome with a sudden clandestine intrigue, and one I couldn't put away. Abruptly, he turned his head and faced me, and as he did I quickly reverted my attention back to my book, hoping he hadn't noticed me peeping at him. But he did, and instantly I knew he was going to say or do something to shoot us out of this peculiar silence. And then he spoke: "What are you reading?"

The tone in his words was innocent, rather uncommon to me, garnished with a husky tint. I didn't respond straight away, rather I pretended to be utterly engrossed in the lines of my book that it took me a few seconds to receive his question, and then, in a rather nonchalant manner, I lifted my head, turned to him and responded, "Enid Blyton."

I kept my eyes on his face for a few seconds, and in doing so studied him for enough time to remember his features. He had a dimple on his left cheek, rather round, beady eyes with large and beguiling pupils, and these boomerang eyebrows that held my attention for a little longer than I'd wanted. Then he scrunched his nose a little, put a finger to his chin and looked up, seemingly lost in rich contemplation.

"Enid Blyton," he said, quizzically, "I've not heard of Enid Blyton." Then he looked down at the book. "Can I see it?"

I didn't want to, but I did want to. And almost mechanically, I gave him the book and watched as he took it into his careful grasp and studied the front and back cover through every corner. Then he flicked through the pages, the thousands of words whizzing before his assiduous concentration, before stopping on one page and reading aloud, "Chapter thirteen, Moon-Face gets into trouble."

Then I saw the course of his gaze skim along the lines of the book with speedy precision before he turned back to me. "Who's this Moon-Face?"

"Well, obviously he's a character," I said, taking back the book, a modest annoyance in my words.

"Could I maybe borrow it when you're done with it?" he asked, innocently.

This question astonished me just a little — it was his forwardness, his keenness to understand what didn't concern him, but also that his question implied that we'd meet again. And I was slightly irked at the thought of lending him my book, but all the while, the fluorescent glint in the smile on his face was beginning to make me feel a little guilty about my unfriendly demeanour, and so I said, with as much composure and respite that I could manage, "Sure."

I opened my book and returned to my page, but I couldn't focus, the tiny grains of subconscious nudges to speak to him engulfed me. So I spoke:

"What are *you* reading?"

Immediately he smiled. "Philosophy!"

Philosophy? I thought. I was aware that such a word existed, but if I had been frank I would have asked him exactly what that complexed-sounding jumble of letters meant and why he was reading it. Instead, I pouted, raised my eyebrows and said, "Oh, nice."

And then he asked me a question that shook my guarding wall and caused a fretful jitter in my stomach:

"Have you read any Philosophy?"

"A little," I lied, looking back down at my book.

"I'm reading about Socrates and Plato. It's my mother's book, she's a philosopher — well, she wants to be one. She doesn't usually let me read these. She says it's too complicated for me. But sometimes I read them anyway."

"And is it?" I asked, still looking down, my eyes catching glimpses of him discreetly.

"Is it what?"

"Too complicated for you?"

He looked down at the book. "I'm not so sure. There are so many words here, but if I try not to think too hard about what they're saying then I think it makes some sense. Want to read some?"

"No thanks," I said, leaning away a little. "It's not my thing."

"How old are you?" he asked.

"Eleven."

"Yeah, you're probably too young."

I huffed. "How old are you?"

"Twelve."

And then silence took the spotlight for a little while, and we found ourselves hidden between the rumbles and buzzes of the cicadas as sunset began to mark its fall over us. Somehow I had found myself ensconced in a stubborn ambivalence: a distinct concoction of uncertainty, certainty, annoyance, scepticism, comfort — an emotional combination uncustomary to me in my youthful naivety of life.

"Do you live around here?" he asked, once again breaking us out of the silence.

"Yes, I live down that way," I said, pointing to a space beyond the distant trees. "My parents own a vegetable farm, and we live there." I looked at his face briefly and his eyes were wide with interest.

"Wow! So you're a farmer?"

"Yes, I am."

"Do you enjoy it?"

So many questions, I thought. "Not really. I'm just used to it. My parents do, I think. Sometimes I get bored and tired of being on the farm all day. That's why I come here."

"I've heard that boredom is just lack of connection," he said, quieter.

I wasn't entirely sure what he meant by that, so I pulled a strange face and pretended not to hear it. I played a little with a strand of my hair frolicking above my eyes as I thought of what to say next.

"Did you just move here?" I asked.

"No, just passing by. Me and Annette, my mother, live in a town in the North - Giverny. She fell in love with a waitress in town here, so we are visiting for some time."

"You call your mother by her name?"

"Yes, don't you?"

"No."

"Oh." He followed a falling leaf with his eyes.

I looked to the ground, then back at him. "She fell in love?"

"Yes, she did," he said, twiddling a strand of grass between his thumb and finger. "Have you ever been in love?"

"Of course not," I replied. "I'm eleven."

I hadn't heard someone speak of the word love with such insouciance, such composure, without the tiniest lilt or quiver in their delivery; there was detachment there, it seemed, or perhaps, thinking back now, speaking of love and things of that nature was normality for him. I couldn't remember ever pondering on a thing such as love, if I had ever felt it, what it could even really be, and I brushed this topic off quite quickly in an attempt to regain a sense of stability and control over what was happening.

"So, for how long will you be staying here?"

"Not sure," he responded quickly. "It all depends on the whims of Annette. She's quite an eccentric person. She says she has this thing of sometimes wanting to be in many places at once. Not sure if that sounds like a gift or a burden."

He spoke funnily, and he was smart, quick-witted, and seemed to contain an effortless sense of astute perception that I vaguely noticed but couldn't place my mind firmly upon. I watched him as he closed his book, leant his head back onto the tree trunk and sighed.

"I've gotta go now," he announced sharply, rolling onto his feet. "Maybe I'll see you here again?"

I looked back down at my book. "Maybe. Though probably not."

"Well, I hope fate works in our favour!"

Weird, cryptic and weird, I thought, and then I listened as he patted away grass from his trousers and jingled the bells on his belt in a springing shake before walking away.

"Vale!" he called.

"Vale?"

"It's goodbye in Latin."

"You know Latin?"

"Only a few words," he said, his voice fading as he left.

Over the page of my book, I stole a quick sight of him walking away, my twinging curiosity getting the better of me. He looked back at me, sending my eyes swiftly back down, but then I looked up again, stealing another glimpse. His stature from behind was getting smaller in the meadow, and somehow I knew he was smiling to himself. Somehow I could feel that from him. Then I allowed myself to fall back into the quietude I had come here for, and as I regained pleasure in my seclusion, I couldn't put away the little probing desire to have him back here, with me, at this pear tree. But I ignored that feeling, and soon fell back into the tale in the pages of my book.

He was there again the following day, leaning up against the trunk, with those little dangling bells, reading another one of his books, philosophy again perhaps. This time I didn't stumble so much when I saw him, and instead I tentatively made my way over to the tree and sat down beside him. As much as I had grown partially fond of him through our previous meeting, I still wasn't sure how I felt about his presence leeching onto my tree, but I went along with it anyway.

"I'm sad today," he pronounced listlessly as I sat by him.

"Why?"

"My dog died a few days ago."

I scratched my chin. "But I saw you yesterday and you didn't seem sad."

He jingled one of his bells. "I think it's only starting to sink in now, this feeling of grief."

I didn't fully understand the hidden messages behind what he spoke, and I sensed he was expecting me to make a comment on this so-called grief he was feeling, but I didn't question it any further in my mind, instead I picked a tiny flower from the grass next to my ankle and handed it to him. "Here."

"Thank you," he said, taking the flower in his twiddling fingers. "He got to experience a lot of fun, anyway, so that makes me feel a little better."

I was just starting to consciously acknowledge the comfort I felt by the timbre of his voice; it sounded tender in youth, just on the edge of teenage blossom, but it twinkled with sincerity, a sincerity that at the time I understood as an alluring sweetness.

"Annette told me that grief is a long journey, a journey that ultimately leads to kindness," he said.

Kindness? I was bemused by his words, yet again, and said, "Well, I hope you feel better soon."

He looked at me. His eyes were watery and emitted hope. I couldn't help but stir in my mind thoughts about the oddness of him as the sound of the wind hit the tree and took the spotlight of our attention for a short while. Then, in a sudden daze, I began humming a melody that I was sure became lost in the wind.

"You like music?" he asked, his voice bubbling just a little with a newfound spark.

"Oh yes, I love music!" I responded enthusiastically. "Folk music especially. What about you?"

"I like jazz."

"Ah, I've never listened to jazz."

"Oh, you must! It's soothing, but it can be chaotic."

"Chaotic, how?" I asked.

"Well, let's see. It shifts, constantly changes. It's kind of like a big mad mess, but it's nice to listen to. Kind of like life. It sounds a lot like life."

How can music sound like life? I wondered. But I didn't speak this thought, instead I started humming again, before catching a fleeting sight of him rocking his head and his feet along to my hums, faded and mercurial as they were. I had always read by this tree, but now I didn't even think about looking down at my book; I was enjoying this too much, even though I still didn't want to admit it. And then, I'm not so sure how, but he smoothly fell into a gush of words, and I listened, because I wanted to. He began talking about the meadow before us, and the beauty of it, the colours and the speckled scatterings of clouds and flowers above and below the fine line of the distance, and how he felt the entire place was here just for the two of us to look out to. I listened to him diverge into a deluge of thoughts coming from springs of his youthful mind, curious but wise for his years, vulnerable and volatile. He told me a little about his world back home, and about how his entire life had changed ever since Annette and the waitress had entered each other's lives. He told me about their meeting: Annette was a writer, a special one, he specified; she'd sit in cafés all the time and get lost in the rows and rows of words with which she'd fill pages. One recent day, on a table by a window in a café on the tip of Provence, the waitress had fortuitously spilt a puddle of coffee onto one of Annette's pages. The waitress immediately apologised, but Annette laughed in a reposeful delight. She had been wrestling with the thought of scrapping that idea and rewriting the page, just waiting for a sign to come along and bear out her conflicting feelings, and this coffee spill had not only done the job but sealed a streak of high-spirited harmony between the two of them. Annette and the waitress took an immediate liking to one another. And how fascinating it was to him, he said, that so much can change from just a singular little instance such as this one, and how easy some things are to miss, but if you are open to the details of a day, something as seemingly insignificant as a little facet of a moment, in this case a splash of coffee, can in fact be hugely significant. I was swept in smoothly by the flow of his stories, and afterwards I told him a little about my own life, about my days and nights on the farm, about my parents, the lifestyle we lived and some patchy anecdotes of the daily activities here and there. He was acutely interested in what I had to say, filled with delicately wild animation in his eyes. And soon after, we fell into a tuneful silence, the fluent breeze blowing on the fabrics of our clothes, turning the pages gently of the book that lay on his lap. In our unspeaking instance, I was thinking about what he said about those little facets, and I understood what he meant. I knew exactly what he was talking about.

Then he turned to me. "So what do you plan to do when you grow up and leave the farm?"

"Leave the farm?" There was a tittering sharpness in my voice. "Why do you suppose I'd want to leave the farm?"

"Oh, do you not?"

"No. Leaving the farm is not something I've ever thought much about. I guess I will take over everything after my parents."

"Is that a wish of yours?"

"Yes." I shrugged my shoulders.

"But you said before that you find it boring, right?"

"I guess anything can be boring. That doesn't mean it isn't the right thing for me."

"You think that?"

"Yes, I do."

And then there became a depth to his smile, a part of him beneath the outer layer that I noticed was trying to decide whether he'd challenge my words and dig deeper, or leave it and let the quiet air be a sudden conclusion. Even though I hadn't known him long at all, I felt that somehow I knew him too well now not to notice the subtle messages behind his countenance. And I wondered if he recognised mine too, or if the stillness of my eyes and the solidity of my mouth guarded my thoughts well enough for them to be hidden. At this point, our conversations seemed quite like a game, a fun frolic of back-and-forth projections. As we turned our attention to a jouncing branch in the tree, he told me about a time, during a trip with Annette to Portugal, they encountered an artist who would tie paintbrushes to the branches of trees and let the wind paint itself onto canvases through the movements of the branches. I was astounded by this. Then I told him about the process of harvesting on the farm, the regimented routines my parents and I lived by, and about our two dogs and seven cats. He smiled along the course of my words. He told me about other philosophers he had read about in his mother's books — Hegel and Nietzsche. He showed me an opal stone he kept inside his pocket, turning it so as to let it flaunt its varied rotation of colours in the sinking sunlight. Then he told me about the art of stone balancing, origami, and purple emperor butterflies. These were things that fascinated him, and through the alacrity behind his bubbly phrasing, they fascinated me too. I told him about my propensity for studying ladybirds, my love for dungarees, and weaving tapestries with my father. Our conversation went on all the way until sunset. He told me about Giverny, about Paris — I had never been to Paris although it had always been a wish of mine — and about places beyond France, places I had dreamed of visiting. And he told me about music concerts, the magic of them, about city cafés, underground trains, art galleries, dancing halls, waterfalls, ancient temples, theatres, things I hadn't yet had the pleasure of experiencing, but things I often thought of when I'd picture the prospect of adventurous discovery. And I wanted to know more, and more, and I prodded him about the things he'd seen and done all the way until the approaching darkness implored me to make my way back home. Nightfall seemed to have come much faster on this evening than any evening I had sat by this tree beforehand. At the time I lacked the eloquence to express this, but I wanted to tell him, as I was leaving, a description of the way I felt; I was inspired, while touched by a sense of pleasant composure, and it was a composure that had reached me only once I had let go of the initial hesitancy to receive his presence, but I just couldn't find the adequate words nor the force in me to get it out, so I let it go. I left, cycling with a satisfied stride all the way home. I hoped I'd see him again as I fell asleep that night, whilst I revisited our conversations in my drifting eyes. And to my happy surprise, I did see him again, almost every day by the pear tree for weeks and weeks. We never planned to meet, but somehow our synchronised timing led us to each other time after time, and after a while it became one of our daily activities to wait there and spend time together in the midst of that special moment between the departing afternoon and the blooming sunset. Leaning up against the pear tree, we'd talk and we'd make jokes and we'd laugh together, sometimes read segments of our books, sing songs the other didn't know, at times we'd sit in silence together, and sometimes I'd tell him stories about my days on the farm, and he'd often tell me stories from his wild and plentiful collections inside his teeming memory bank. He would leave Provence eventually, he occasionally reminded me, but I didn't think it would be soon, or perhaps, thinking back, I refused to let my mind go to the scenes of his incoming departure, and instead I chose to enjoy the companion I had made and the special transience it would inevitably be. With these days, the pear tree, formerly my own, had become ours, *our* pear tree. Sometimes I'd see him for many days in a row, other times not for a few days, and just when I would begin to think he'd left for good and I'd face the approaching edge of a sinking sadness, he'd show up again, leaning up against the trunk with a book in his hands and a buoyant smile on his face. Still, he'd remind me that it was only a matter of time before Annette would spontaneously pack their bags and they'd set off, but I still chose not to think too much about all of that. I was sure he could tell I was becoming accustomed to him, and by reminding me I knew he wanted to spare me some disappointment, and perhaps himself too. But he told me he'd visit, eventually, that here by this tree, with me, was a special place that he would hold onto even on his distant travels. Then one day, he vanished. It was a haunting surprise. I waited for him day after day after day until I slowly began to expect his absence, and although a quiet hope for him remained in me, he did not return. Months passed by and there was no sight of him. Eventually, the pear tree became my own secluded spot again, and things went back to the way they had been before he showed up, although it was a long time before the serenity of merely sitting and reading there alone had returned, untainted by longing. The hope of him eventually faded into a small, delicate wish that floated in the background, but it lingered, nevertheless. And, as dispiriting as it may sound, I never saw him again. Occasionally I would dip into worrisome thoughts, creating unpleasant scenarios about what could have happened to him, and then, with the passing of more time, I stopped thinking about him much at all; he became a subject of thought that would vault up with a triggered remembrance, such as at the sight of a bell, at the word philosophy, or those random instances where deep-seated memories lurch into one's consciousness as though a hidden button has been pressed behind the mind's eye. That was what he became to me. He faded, and faded, until he became a fragment, made up of particular distinct memories, broken and fractured and withered in colour and tone, but still a part of me nonetheless.

So, I must bring you back here, forwards twenty years, to today, on the rainy corner of a block down the road from Avenue Montaigne. The light entrance of the afternoon was steering in. I was passing by a bakery that caught my sight in a glimpse. I thought I'd pick up some loaves of bread and perhaps some raspberry jam. Inside, through the flare of the orange sun and the fog of flour dispersing from the bread the baker threw onto the shelves, I spotted something that brought me to a halt and triggered a surge of some elusive substance, amorphous and visceral, to come gushing through and out of me. One, two, three, four, five — five bells hung from the belt of loose-fitting jeans on someone who stood not too far away. My eyes trailed upwards through the fluffs and broken cotton threads of a cardigan, but the face was obscured by the light. I stepped round a countertop, my head tilting with unshackled curiosity, until the light moved away and caused the shadows to reveal the lineaments of a face. Kind features, I thought, a face with a salient familiarity. I walked a few inches closer, surreptitious in my steps. Then I saw, with the angular raise of someone lost in deliberation at the sight of bread, two eyebrows curved with the tilt of a boomerang. It was his face. My eyes stopped seeing everything else, and upon tracing each and every outline of his in a glut of just a few seconds, I felt my heart widen. I let out a quiet, humorously stupefied chuckle. He seemed to be in a rush, clocking his eyes onto the shelves of bread in speedy lines, his fingers fluttering over the wide selection. I couldn't refrain from staring at him as I walked by. Then he looked at me, a slight disconcertion on his expression, fused with a feather-light whimsicality. He smiled speedily, and nodded, before looking back at the bread and taking a bunch into his arms. I turned away. I was feeling every layer of unbelievability, but unsure of how to act on such sensations. I grabbed some loaves of bread, headed to the counter and stood behind him. He paid the baker with a friendly charm before heading out. With haste, I paid and followed out the door behind him. I was inundated with a cloudburst of excitement and conflicting emotions, too engulfed in this rippling fusion along with the sound of speeding cars and the tumult of determined passersby for me to regain my bearings. Say something to him, anything, I kept thinking to myself assertively. But for reasons that befuddled me, I didn't — he was too focussed, briskly headed out the entranceway. Here outside, the rain was pouring with heavy precision. He stepped right out into it from under the awning. There was a car parked on the road and a hand was waving out to him, and he waved back before speeding up to make it to the car. I walked right behind him, and though I could not find a single word to say I must have made a sound and he must have heard me because he turned around to face me. He nodded once more, a slight confusion on his face as to who I was and why I was following him. I looked into his eyes, my mind racing with a wild emptiness.

"Vale," I uttered in a hurried whisper, my words breaking through the rain.

The word had come in a sudden piercing memory. It was all I could think to say. He remained looking at me, his footsteps slowing down. Droplets of mighty rain fell onto his widening eyes as his face became an expression of sincere reminiscence, of a heartfelt warmth, a curling, blazing fire of wild happiness. The voice from the car called his name, and he turned to look at them, then back at me, and then he smiled gently. "Vale."

RANI'S BUCKET

How odd, how strange. Her stillness glows, her head rocks with the current of an imperceptible sway to solid water. She is tired from years, gaunt with age, and she is unnoticed, unheard, her presence shakes no one, her voice wobbles and reaches not a single soul. Her hair is white, radiant as the ring around the moon, and her soft vesture hangs with the ageless grace that binds her shallow breath. But how odd, how incredibly strange. She stares into the darkness beyond the window as though a friend sits opposite and the two of them communicate through a telepathic cord. She seems to have cut ties with time; a minute to her would be a meaningless sound, an hour a gentle breeze. She seems to glide through time, as opposed to everyone else who scurries behind it; perhaps her relationship with time has resulted in mutual indifference, for they have lived with one another for so long that they've gone their separate ways; but they respect each other, her and time, from a metaphysical distance. I wonder what she would say if she were to see me, me and my fascination that flows towards the uncovering of her and her disposition, the person she conveys, her self-invented communication with which she demonstrates the way she knows to live. I think perhaps I know you, or rather, I've known you, from a place that isn't here, but was, or it could be that in you I see glimpses of me, maybe that could be it, but it doesn't really matter from where fascination stems, for you are familiar to me in a way I suppose I'll never understand. And I hope someday we meet, I hope we do.

Why don't you move? I can't even trace the subtle dance of your breath, at least not from this distance. If I drew nearer to you perhaps I'd see it; perhaps I'd be able to trace the line of movement your chest draws in the air, ignited with life through the curving of your summit that is lit by the ceramic lamp on your windowsill. Why must walls curtail us now? You don't know me, you haven't seen me, but I've seen the shape of you, still and inconsolable like a hushed whisper that wishes never to grow. You are my secret — can I be yours? Is it odd to think this way? It must be. So then oddity must be a gift of nature.

Today I see you in your front garden as I walk by. You are trying to pull the weeds but the feebleness in your limbs gets in the way. I can't help but watch you. I watch you with a keen focus, with the intrigue of a star's light, with the persistence of time's mutability, with a certain attention I have only ever found in the eyes of lovers. And you don't see me, but today I quite like that, I quite like seeing the steadiness in the undisturbed inspection of your shaded eyes, and though your hands and your knees tremble in little intermitted tremors, the concentration you contain is that of a funambulist. It's as if you hold an occult wisdom of merely being alive, and you do it so simply. You are there and I am here. I cannot get to you, I cannot billow into your world, unless I make a gesture of some sort, or maybe a sound — then would you see me trying to see you? You tend to the garden with the slowness in the final act of a slumber; your faltering hands do not notice they falter; your white hair is fumbling in the helical autumn wind. I've noticed your struggle. Is there anything you need? Is there anything I could do to chisel the edges of your day? Surely you could do with some help with these weeds; they outnumber those slow hands of yours. Could I offer *my* hands? Could I offer you a pair to get through them all? Should I ask you if you need some help? I think I will ask you — and so I ask. I ask you if I could be of any service to you, but it seems that my words do not reach you. I wonder, do you hear only with your touch? I ask you again, and then you look at me. Your eyes are rounder now that they face me, and they seem to have become lighter, lit with the simple gesture of a small captured enquiry. You say nothing at all, but you smile with the slightest hesitation between your brows. I ask you once more. You look down to your soil-ridden hands, then to me, and then you nod with a gradual but grateful shimmer of the head. Yes, you say, yes, you would love to accept my offer. Your voice is on the edge of brittleness, but it reflects a soundless temperament of purity, a place from where you send your tender currents out to the world, no ounce of pretence, no shade of guile. And so we weed. You bend with the waste, I with the knees. We tend to this garden with the joined force of our fingers, together; I pull from where it strains you to reach, I crouch under the shrub that gets in your way, I get my hands beneath where yours will not allow you; and I notice the way you notice this, with the same recognition that pours over the face that receives cherished gifts of affection. You are so frail, so fragile and slow, infirmity has swallowed you, yet you seem to see things with a gaze agape, with a sensibility that towers, never fumbles, embalmed by the infinity of time.

The sun has set over us and I notice that you are bereft of even the smallest slither of energy, that to make your way back inside is now a trying manoeuvre, so I take your hand and give you some of my strength and stamina, and we walk unhurriedly into the shadows of your home. At first I feel intrusive, but then I find that you seem to want me here, you seem to value my fellowship, for you offer me tea and a seat by the warmth. Of course, I would love nothing more than to have tea with you, I tell you, but I shall brew it, and you shall sit. I watch you fall with a heavy sigh into the body of the wing chair, the one that faces the window, your tired face thawing into the homely air that allows space for every satisfactory breath. I stand by the wooden counter and look at the back of your rested head, at you, you merely living in your silence, without any haste to please me, or to attune the space to my sudden arrival, untainted by anything of that sort, and you look straight through the window where the outline of the sycamore tree is built by the glare of a growing night light outside on the pavement. I watch it too, wondering why you are so infatuated. When the kettle resounds, I brew us the lapsang souchong that sits on the countertop, and then I pull out a chair and sit beside you, facing the window. I want to look out with you, to see what you see. The rising steam from the tea twirls upwards in a disorderly manner, marking a dance of white angelic snakes at the fore of the dim world outside that thin sheet of glass you so fluently behold. And then I see it arrive — an owl, brown and frosted with white patches, resting on the branch in front of the window. Its penetrating, honey-coloured eyes seem to form a line that spears the glass, clasping onto your vivid centre. It sits like a master, an arbiter of the night. I turn to look at you. Your expression is now shooting rays of contentedness, as though you've found what you have been looking for. I have become merely a spectator, a prying witness crouching to see through a tiny rift the bond between you and this fine owl. I am not here anymore, I cannot be, for I am not made of the vital elements that would allow me to be a component of this connection; I am entirely different, an outsider, an admirer with no vessel to become involved. I look back and forth — you, the owl, you, the owl, you — and somewhere between the zone of the both of you I find a particle that is me, swimming, wallowing in the lenient gravity that lies in the liminal area that the two of you have invented.

The outside has reached its threshold of darkness. The owl flies away and I hear you sigh with delight as you lean back a little. You stare ahead and I start to think that you've forgotten I am here, but then you breathe out a hum that forms into a sweet glissando and you point towards the two cups of tea that have been sitting on the small table in front. Swinging out of my reverie, I pick up the tea that has become tepid, but neither of us seem to care, and together we sip with slow, inconspicuous tilts of our hands, mindfully rested here together. Soon our cups hold nothing, and the chirping sounds of the night rise from the window as though shifting through a sound tunnel and dispersing into limitless depths with the out-growing curve of the tunnel walls. You and I, we are here. I've seen you from the disconnected view of my own home, and now I am within the borders of yours, with you. I want to say something. I want to speak to you. I tell you how safe I feel. You cough a little into your weightless hand and then turn to me, and after your eyes have found mine, you ask me what my name is. I tell you my name, and then I ask for yours. Rani, you say. I observe the frailty in your voice, broken with the weathering of a hundred years. You sigh and then gently close your eyes, and I watch your eyelids fall with the movement of a departing tide. You draw breath in, rumbling through the croaks of your throat, and then you tell me, slowly, that your withering memory urges you to forget much of the life you've lived. I look at you, attempting to capture the tone of your character that now exudes nothing but mystery. You seem as though you've been summoned to a place between the waves of joy and despair, faltering between the harmony of both sides, but merged with the mixture of each of their complex natures. I wish not to forget it, you say, I wish not to forget it, you say again in an almost indecipherable whisper. I lean closer to you. Forget what? I ask. You breathe in. When you were a child, you tell me, you lived under a tin roof, and whenever it rained, beneath its slanting body, you'd sit and listen to the millions of pouring droplets. In them you found tiny signs of the world, a place where you could make sense of things through a divine sound that poured over you. I listen to you stammer through your story, and I am dumbfounded by the colour in each syllable you pronounce, the euphonic quiver hidden between the threads of your quiet phrasing. This sound, you say, cloaked your entire childhood, and underneath this sound were the memories of your unfledged years. You wish not to forget the sound of rain on the tin roof, you say, you wish not to forget it. Stumbling through a breath, you tell me that you used to be a painter, someone who cast the life of merging colour onto bare spaces; you painted the world you saw with your eyes closed. And your hands, you say as you lift them delicately above, shaking and slow, fragile in space like aged leaves engaging with the torrid air; you say they have somehow forgotten the movement of the brush, those fathomless swirls you pursued, that somehow the memory has been stolen by the disappearing years. You wish not to forget it, you tell me. You wish not to forget the taste of the walnut cake your grandmother baked on every birthday of yours in the bloom of your growth. And your favourite song, you say, leaning in the bend of a hazy thought, Hejira, you wish not to forget the fading sound of that song, the song you cherished for many distant decades, the song that has sadly evaporated from the retention of your ears. It sounds as though caterpillars rest on your tongue, for you speak now with a slurred delivery. You tell me that many years ago you lived by the Aegean sea, and that you've started to forget the feeling of sinking your feet into sand, a sensation you met time and again when you'd sit by the shore and stand mighty and high before the ballad of the waves. You wish not to forget it, you say. And then your head falls downwards as you keep on whispering. I wish not to forget it. I wish not to forget it. I find that I am enraptured by the cascade of your sadness and your hope, tarnished by numerous years, slowly uttered through your fading mouth, how each word escapes from you in small, hushed leaps but arrives with the thump and impact of a heart with the drum of the world seething through its chorus. You are so rested, engraved by the repose of closed eyes and dim lights, unperturbed by me and the noise of my alertness. You seem to glide through each moment, allowing the slow currents of what arrives to take you with them. But you can't help but reminisce, can you? You can't help but long for the touch, the taste, the smell of what once lived within you as you hold the awareness of your transience, steering closer to a new beginning, an ultimate forgetting. You seem to look forwards with the steady solidity that blesses mountains, but all the while a part of you longs for what was, a part of you meets the narrow feeling of limitation, of being in the descent of what no longer exists. You covet the backwards tilt in the swing of time, you are meeting the tide in the sea of loss, but you face it with the gentleness of transitioning seasons, a lightness cast above this heavy humanity in which we find ourselves wrapped. You fall asleep and I look up to the ceiling, set up tall with plasterboard, a substance that, unlike tin, rejects the heart of rain by reducing its unfeigned reverberation. And soon it will rain, but you, Rani, will not hear it the way you wish to. And I find that to be a sad thought. I see you rested in a deep cave, some place I can no longer find you, and so, gently, I get up and leave you. But I think to myself, as I walk away and close the door softly behind me, soon I will see you again.

Now a week has passed. Tonight, at the immediate touch of dusk I will knock on your door. I have prepared something for you, a gift, for how could I not? I have been affected, greatly affected by our small time together that I've felt a summoning of insight, an idea that came to me initially with a quiet sign, but one I sat with and let grow in the nest of my thoughts. I am enthusiastic, I am feverish with the spring of a cat's tail beneath my feet; I am eager to meet you tonight, and I will take this feeling with me to your door. And when I do, I knock, knock, knock, my knuckle moving with the throb of a zealous infant. I wait a minute, and when you open the door I see that your eyes are now lit with the same flicker of light that appears at the rendezvous with the owl, but now this light is directed at me, and I am overjoyed to see it. In one hand I carry some weighty paper bags, and in the other I hold a shiny bucket. You welcome me in with gracious eyes and I enter your home. You walk tonight with the same slowness of our previous meeting, but there is a weightlessness in the tremble of your steps tonight; you are meeting the ground as though it is a cloud just about dense enough to hold the silent weight of you. I pull out a chair for you and I brew you tea. It is lapsang souchong again, your favourite, I presume. You sit and look towards me. I notice, through the smoothness collapsing over your brows, that you do not question my being here, you simply sit comfortably in the combined reality we have set for ourselves, in the knowledge that we are together now, and there is nothing else. Again, I sit beside you and together we drink the tea. How wonderful it is to be here once more, clustered in a serenity you know so well, and it is quite a particular serenity, and one that I have found in only a few rare corners. Together, we have found the encompassing element of peace; I am like a shy wind, you are like a lily of the valley, dulcet and pendent, eloquently living whilst I discover your special circumference with a soundless contact, out of sight and in the air we have merged between us. When all of the tea has been drunk, you remain still. I get up and out of one of the bags I take out a large enclosed ebony box that I place on the ground by your feet. Then I unlock it and turn over the lid. Inside there is sand, small heaps of sand, sand I have collected from the beach. I drove a long distance, across the city and through rows of suburban towns to get to the coast, and I've brought them here, to you. I don't know how many grains lay within those little wooden walls, but I hope there are enough there to ignite the feeling your feet have longed to feel. I kneel beside you. Your smile exudes a hushed mesmerism. Delicately, I remove your socks and place your feet inside the box, on top of the sand, each grain seized from the ocean's border to meet you. I look at your feet settling into the cold granulose sensation, and then your toes, digging tiny holes into the pores of the soft grit. You laugh, first from a small, inward gasp, and then out to a great heap of trailing chuckles. A loud remembrance is written in every sound you make, every intricate circle your toes draw. Out of another bag, I take out a hand-sized cassette deck and a cassette tape that I insert into the deck, side A. Immediately, a small fuzzy hiss and a muffled crackle disperse before the song begins. The guitar, the bass, muted by the limited frequency of the speaker, but containing a fluid slew of melody trickles outwards. Its whisper is ageless, effortless. I see you hear the song, your eyes widening, but you do not move a limb; you are waiting for the sound to pour into you. Then you begin to mime the shape of the lyrics, your mouth chasing the words, reunited with certain details that had slipped away from you a long time ago. The music weeps and rolls through you, and you close your eyes as though they'll never need to reopen. An indelible affection lies in the corner of the indentation beside your fruitful smile. I can do nothing but stand and watch you, you with your hovering chin and your slanting eyebrows, with a scintilla of joy in every shape your lips form, you who are restoring the pictorial sense of something so cherished that had been lost, who pulls the sunken treasure from beneath the multilayered ground. You seem as though you are lost within the greatest thoughts. You mime the words: we're only particles of change, I know, I know, orbiting around the sun, but how can I have that point of view when I'm always bound and tied to someone? And I notice you are crying. You cry so wonderfully. It is a pure cry. I think your eyes are a channel through which the great liquid salt of nature can travel, and you do not know it, no, you do not know the sincerity of your tears, and that is what makes your cry the pure cry that it is. When the song closes, you place your hands in the air, and they are shaking with enervation and with a passion too large for them to contain. You turn to look at me. You are telling me with your kind eyes that you are thankful. I look to you with vivid intention. Oh, but there's more, I say to you. I bend down, and out of another bag I take out a triangular-shaped thing wrapped in cloth and twine and I unravel a fine slice of cake with little shattered walnuts on the top. I present the slice to you. Your expression now expands to an unfaltering excitement, narrow by weakness but so unrestrained, and with a grandness that transgresses every era of life. With a fork, I break off a piece, and then you open your mouth, and I feed it to you, every crumb succumbing to your devotion. No sooner does the taste enter the first layer on your tongue than the lights of your mind switch off and before you opens an entrance to a hallway of a stark remembrance through which you are catapulted and sent to a single ember of thought, a paroxysm in every grain of distant recollection. I am certain that behind those sweetly wrinkled eyelids, the tiny dotted elements that make up your pupils have rebuilt themselves to be those of your much younger self, closer in imagination than even we are in physicality. You are dreaming through the fine capturing of a taste, so distinct to you in its specificity that I am no longer concerned how far off I have missed the mark of capturing the flavour flourished by your grandmother's loving hands. I place my palm on your shoulder and you place yours on top of mine as you absorb even the minutest crumb. You have untangled the thread of an irretrievable past. You have traversed the tick of the clock. You are nothing but the taste of the walnut cake. Then, once you've opened your eyes, I put aside the plate, and from another bag I take out an oval plywood pallet, and on the pallet I squeeze little circles of colour from tubes of paint. Then I take out a paintbrush, the bristles straight and pristine, and I hand it to you. Again, I crouch down to the bag and from it I take out a small canvas, untouched and bright with unbound potential. I stand in front of you. In one hand I hold the pallet, in the other the canvas. Now, on your face, there is an ambience that reaches beyond the furthest fields of my vision. You seem as though you are seeing through the mist of a dream, but with a substance that carves a glisten on the edges of everything, that allows you to see this canvas along with the poignancy and immediacy of everything it could be. You dip the paintbrush into the paint. I watch your hand empower the bristles and summon forth the colours. Then you lift the paintbrush in the air and mark a trail onto the canvas. You lead the paintbrush to sway between the paint, the canvas, the paint, the canvas. You are conjuring the detail of the finest embroidery with every movement of your harmonic rotation. I do not know how much time passes for I too am carried along the lines of the shapes you forge, but when you stop and sit back and I feel it is complete and I turn the canvas to see what you've painted, I see nothing but an outflow of you, Rani, a wise arabesque holding an essence that mirrors a picture of your ageless vulnerability. You are enlivened by a tremendous gust that you once knew. I see it in every inch of you. You are a newly hatched creature that sits before the great sky and loses the sense of itself at such a sight, and so it too holds the magnificence of this all-embracing beauty. I brew more tea for us. We must wait, I tell you. So we sit together and drink. I notice that you are speechless, that your mind hasn't quite the capacity in the moment to awaken what you feel, but your silence projects it all, your silence emits nothing but a fulfilled appetite that has longed for a wildly familiar grasp of living. And your smile deepens with each minute that passes us. And finally, when I hear what begins as specks of unapparent taps on the window and quickly culminates into a downpour of vigorous rain, I stand and take your hand in mine. You are so determined to follow me that you rise to your feet with a slow burst of contagious vibrancy. With the other hand I grab the bucket, tapping playfully on the shimmering tin as I lead you to the door. When I open the door the wind sends a splatter of rain over us. You laugh, and through your laughter I find my own, and so we laugh together. With slow footsteps, I lead you out to the front garden. You stand there, waiting to be a part of whatever I will now conduct, rain sprinkling all over your hair and dripping along the lines of your cheeks. I carefully place the bucket over your head, all the way over, holding the rim just above your shoulders. Listen, I say to you, unsure if my words have made it through the torrent and the tin. And behind the tin bucket that obstructs me from capturing a glimpse of whatever it is your face currently exudes, behind it I hear the playful hum of a sprouting life, of someone new to the world, so susceptible to its wonders and not yet stirred by its adversities. You are living in your very own purity at this second, and it's a purity that is always there even when you do not know it, a purity that emerges to you through something so particular: an odd, a strange, but brilliant thing like the sound that now fervently meets you. The rain proceeds to collide with the tin. I watch each droplet fall in and around one another on the bucket. There it is. Right there. There is that sound you wished not to forget. There it is, Rani, there it is.

ALCOVE OF SWIFT CAPRICE

I was in a semi-drowsy state before I stepped onto this balcony, swept outside by a keen urge to immerse myself in the coldness here and write something, anything. Now I'm sitting here, pen on a notepad which rests on my lap, tea on the octagonal table to my left, with a bit of a jitter inside my stomach. But at last, I can feel the gale again. The notepad on which I write is old and worn, and on the first handful of pages are scattered scribbles and writings from a hand I have never known. I found it stored away in the little room underneath the staircase, under a forest of collected dust; it must have been here long before me, waiting for someone to discover its lonely shape among the shadows. I wanted to write to someone after realising that I hadn't written a letter in a long while. I want to access that place where the hand moves rhythmically along the course of an exploratory mind, drawing words because it must. I think writing can be an exercise of no control, and sometimes it's exactly the thing that is needed to pull out those little pips lodged in the back of your psyche. So here I am, writing to you. Who you are, I'm not even so sure. I was thinking perhaps you are a friend, a relative, an old teacher, my neighbour whose tender footsteps I often hear, or the person I met in the bar last week, whose name was Julian. Or maybe you are all of these people, and myself, all of us ensnared into the graphite of this self-possessed pencil. Now I want to tell you that just as I dotted the end of the previous sentence I witnessed a cat jump from the fence that borders the front garden of the building facing me and straight up and through the open window of the first floor flat. I watched it stop suddenly and soften into a brief pause before taking that massive leap; I guess in that fraction of a second it was contemplating such a mighty jump, analysing the potential risks, the chance of not making it, the shape it needed to assume to dive in with such sharp precision. Cats — those nimble creatures always astound me, with their stupefyingly precise movements and character that most of the time gives a care for nothing other than repose. Anyway, back to where I was getting at, which I'm not sure has a fixed location, but instead falls into a motion similar to the whim of an underwater current. What I wish to write here is, I presume, going to come out of me with the quickness and acuteness of going down a slide, and as strange as that sounds, somehow it makes perfect sense to me. Before I stepped out here, I was falling asleep on the sofa, listening to Nina Simone pour out her soul on the stage to a large crowd of admirers who clapped and cheered whenever she gifted them a space of time. I was thinking how magical it must have been to be in the room there, with her and her mind and music ablaze, enamoured of such a breathtaking song. Even from the radio speaker the music approached me with this quietly powerful impact, nonchalantly striking. And what she was singing of — human care, rekindling feelings of love, beauty — wheedled me into a state of equanimity. And then she struck the keys of the grand piano, abruptly, with the immediacy of a storm, forcing my attention on the virtuosic glitters of travelling chords she played so effortlessly, chord after chord after chord. And I began thinking: what an adventure, what an adventure-seeker she is; she seeks and finds and then seeks again, folding over every single layer she can get her hands on to execute a remarkable story. I closed my eyes and thought to myself: this, this transcends genre. And when I got up from the sofa, in some kind of whirlwind of awe, I looked at your painting, Maya, the one you gave me last autumn. Wild expressionism. I had seen it in my periphery every day but somehow hadn't seen it in this way before; I noticed the adventure in it, the trails after strokes after colours melting into a journey to some majestic liquid atmosphere. I think painting, colour in fact and the fusion of it, has a way of communicating to us what we know deeply but can't express, for how can I translate the colour green into another form? How can I accurately articulate the difference between yellow and blue? And, I think the purple intermingling with the red in this work of art brings forth a sort of reminiscence, a rekindling of a forgotten message: the innate pursuit of adventure. I think, perhaps I have lost some of this for some time, or maybe "lost" is a strong word, and in fact I've been out of touch with this part of myself for a while. And I think I'd like to reacquaint myself with it. Anyway, I then became drowsy with oscillating thoughts and that's why I stepped outside to write, but I've mentioned that already. Suddenly my mind jumps to you, Anura, you with your wide eyes open to the currents of the day. The silhouette of hair in the window beside me reminds me so much of yours, the way it sits like falling water. I would love nothing more than time in your company again; we always have the greatest moments together. Do you remember when we jumped over the gate to that private garden in that strange neighbourhood of the inner city, and how I had to help you down after you got stuck at the top? We whisper-laughed with glistening tears in our eyes while trying to keep our voices down. But of course we couldn't help ourselves. Do you remember when we stayed in the river cottage, and that morning when we tried to make chai tea and we opened the cupboard door and heaps of cinnamon fell onto our hair, and how we laughed as we dusted each other off? And these are only memories that come to me now; there are many more, so many more. Do you remember the jar of ginger and mint tea we brewed for Bonne when he had a fever and how we cycled in the rain in the streetlamp-lit town to bring it to him? And Bonne, I remember brightly our days in Berlin, tucked away in that tiny apartment between the art house and the sushi shop and the wild neighbour who would sweep the public hallway with a garden broom before the first glint of sunrise. We barely had money to afford anything, but still, I remember this time with so much fondness because we could share our misfortunes with each other, and somehow find comfort and at times hilarity in it. We'd laugh about not being able to afford to eat out, while we watched through the window all the people wining and dining in those extravagant restaurants, and instead we'd cook at home and eat whatever we could find — forgotten strips of spaghetti, vegetables that we weren't even sure were vegetables, tins of whatever happened to be inside, hidden stashes of chocolate. I remember one day sitting on the sofa with you, hands on our stomachs laughing while we jokingly wished that money was some sort of cosmic currency, along with more otherworldly scenarios we created in our dream-dazed minds. And I love how we'd encourage each other's creative endeavours — me with your compositions and you with my writing. I remember an evening I was feeling disheartened about a project I was working on. You sat with me and told me that it's easy for someone to devalue their own ideas because they are with their own thoughts all the time, and you told me to try to recognise my own insightfulness, my own wisdom, the same way I recognise it in others. I don't remember if I told you but those words were exactly what I needed to hear that night. Now, back to that adventure I was speaking of. I remember, as a child, those occasional weekends when I'd stumble into my mother in the kitchen, way after midnight. We'd both happen to still be awake and craving a nighttime snack. I remember precisely that "you're still awake?" she'd say to me in a whisper that broke with astonishment and delight to see me. Together we'd quietly peruse the cupboards in search of a snack, giggling as we tried to keep the noise down. There would always be some erratic thing to playfully discuss, like the distant snoring, or how we both hated the condiment that had been in the fridge for far too long, or why the cupboards were so awfully squeaky. And there was always that distinct feeling between us that we'd unknowingly create together, that feeling of collaborative enthusiasm our murmurs would give life to. We had found each other in that special interlude, outside of the regimes and the structures of the day, and right there we would engender a true spirit of adventure. That's the feeling. Now, suddenly I'm pulled to wistful memories, of childhood, of adolescence. Ah, the alcove — that's a memory I haven't paid a visit to in a long time. When I was a child, I'd often visit the home of my close friend, and in this home was an alcove, a huge alcove in the wall. The family always spoke of installing padded seating there — I'm certain they never did — but my friend and I would often sit there together, in the emptiness that was ours. It became a sort of hideaway for us, a place where we'd find shelter and whisper torrents of stories and fantasies. Eventually we decided it was a special place, an alcove unlike any other, and the effect of this alcove unfolded into a phantasmagorical one. We could not step into it without unearthing a hidden adventure upon stepping out; each time we'd step out, the room had to change in one way or another, and it always did. I'm sure there is some faded information that I'm missing to explain precisely how it worked, but the alcove became a place we would go to when we wished to pull ourselves out of the formulaic arrangements of the day and foster an awakening of limitless thrill. And we'd return, and we'd return, and again, we'd return. It's getting colder and my hand is starting to quiver just a little, but something just popped into my mind, something I feel I must write about — a moment I witnessed the other day, on the bus. A child was sitting in front of me, and next to this child sat an older guardian, presumably a grandparent. I heard the child ask the grandparent what the day was, and they responded, "Today is Thursday." Then the child let out a heave of a sigh filled with discontentment and asked, "Is it possible to change the day?" The grandparent chuckled, and responded, "Why would you want to change the day?" "Well," the child replied, "I want it to be Saturday. On Saturday the days are always fun. There is no fun on Thursday." The grandparent lovingly stroked the child's head and said, "Then fun is only two days away." I smiled at this small interaction, and as I stared into the passing panorama outside I replayed the conversation in my mind. And then I thought, no, today can indeed be Saturday, if that is what you wish for. Days. I think perhaps we give the names of days too much power. During my years at school, after I had been thoroughly introduced to the system of the week, I often saw each day as an individual character, each containing specific traits whether I enjoyed them or not. Oh, Monday, must you be so hasty and repetitive? Must you push forth your lines and lines of regulations so ruthlessly? Tuesday was always a little better, Wednesday even a little better,

Thursday was just as disheartening as Monday and I had never known why, and Friday was the cheerful friend with words of aspiration. Saturday was always a mystery, and Sunday, no matter what was happening, could rarely be a day of exuberance, Sunday was always a day to be slow. But why must we fit life into these repetitive compartments, constantly expecting the same seven outcomes? Perhaps we are just too habituated to whatever it is we have decided that each day feels like, we are familiar with the emotional patterns, we know how to feel, what to expect, and we aren't completely open to the spontaneity of what could arrive if we just let each day be a blank canvas. And maybe what I'm writing here is a letter like the many I've written and found no use for, filled with musings that tomorrow will have no true purpose. But for now these thoughts feel relevant. And at least now I know I am not the only recipient. So, child on the bus, today is Saturday, and so is every day if that's what you wish for. The opportunity for the fun you seek is always here, and here, and here. And for me, today is not the day that it is, today is in fact a brand new day, a day that has truly never before existed. And today I will go into the alcove, yes, today I will go into the alcove.

PRETTY FROCKS IN A VIOLENT WIND

The candlelight lives brazenly beside us as we lay on the fluffs
of the rug, plump cushions beneath our heads, knitted
blankets to our chins. Our eyes are slowly drifting, but we are
still awake, not sure how close or far we are from sleep.
Should we leave the candle burning for now? Should we wait
a little longer until we are on the brink of melting away? I
think we should leave it, yes, let's leave it, and then we can
blow it out when we feel ourselves sinking. This is a pleasant
feeling, to be here. Those windows beside us, we are not
certain about what lies beyond them for we have never
roamed these roads before; they could display a world of
anything at this minute. I wonder what will happen tomorrow.
I wonder what awaits. Maybe tomorrow the leaves of
generous trees will swish open like stage curtains and reveal a
place of many lands, too plentiful to count, and many paths,
many doors and details. And we'll have time, we'll have all
the time to wander through. We breathe in, we breathe out.
We are talking through mouths that are almost sealed. Ideas
are slipping on the surface of our minds, falling through a
doorway that exists on the tip of a dream. We are drifting,
going away, but we are still here, still in that place where the
fine thread of a delicious slumber is held back by determined
imagination. Our words seem to come from an inner
landscape, sprung out through our resting voices, and our
awareness of what we say is sinking slowly, but we speak,
nonetheless, even if it is only within the bounds of half-
fledged words. Together we are a lighthouse, shining a fading

beacon in the final minutes of darkness. In the morning, perhaps we'll wake to the scent of tea leaves, and we'll open the window and let the bountiful tassels of air enter this abode. We'll sit on the credenza and feel the outside inviting us. Then we'll step out, and the warm wind will tease the tiny hairs on our arms, and we'll go, we'll leave like the previous minute that silently slipped away. Perhaps we will find a hidden street with much to see, or a place to sit that's built upon a tree, or we'll encounter a secret den where we'll learn to sculpt, to mould shapes with our hands. We'll eat in the park by a herd of deer. You'll tell me something about deer, something I've never heard, something that will make me want to stay there longer and watch the way they exist. Perhaps we'll cross a bridge, and on the other side we'll meet someone, someone with glasses shaped as the crescent moon, and with eyelashes like whiskers, yes, they'll have eyelashes like whiskers and rose-coloured dungarees. They'll show us their favourite place, and it will be a place we won't want to leave, so we won't, we'll stay there for as long as we please, and a celebratory air will be there with us. We'll joke, and you'll laugh wildly, brilliantly. You'll glaze the scenes that pass with your humour, and you'll cross the threshold with your eccentric ideas. Then our whiskered friend will pull out a musical instrument, a guitar, no, a dulcimer, and we'll slip into a song, all three of us, then four, then five. More people will join, and we'll all sing together, and I'll occasionally look at you to acknowledge the extraordinary moment into which we have surprisingly wandered. We'll talk to those around us, characters of plentiful shades. We'll encounter someone named Beth, Beth will be her name, Beth who sells grapes in a stool that was handed down to her from her ancestors. She will be the spirit of the party, but when we settle down she'll share with us her great dilemma, that she feels deep down there's more out there for her than the grape stool, but she also wishes dearly to carry on the legacy of her predecessors, that, and she's passionate about grapes. We'll console her, and she'll give us heaps of grapes, grapes that burst and yield puddles of marvellous juice. We'll eat them under the sunset. We'll eat again, in a place where fire crackles in the corner and charming rugs lay over floors of warped wood, and stacks of books and kokeshi dolls are lined up on the shelves. Someone in a red tuxedo will be playing an old pipe organ in the corner, galloping along the circle of fifths. Now my eyes are closed, are yours? The candle still burns, and its flicker seems to approach with dull shadows swimming over our eyelids in silhouettes of infinite curves. I don't want to blow it out, not yet. A sweet-looking elderly lady who sits alone in the corner with her eyes closed will remind me of my grandmother. I'll tell you that. Then I'll tell you about my grandmother and her box sets, her box sets of videotapes. She would always listen. She would never watch them and I never knew why. Her eyes were always closed, just listening. She would sit there, seemingly asleep, but always awake, often smiling when it was funny, her eyebrows often raising into small hills when it was serious. I used to wonder if she preferred to see it play out in her head, if that was much more gratifying to her, to draw out the images herself. But I don't know why. It was always a curious little thing to me. You'll smile. You'll tell me something to do with videotapes, something like you had an old French teacher who owned a vast collection of them, and that he'd get you to watch stacks of French films from directors whose names you only vaguely remember, and you'll tell me that you always found inspiration in them, they always gave you a little something to carry with you. Our conversations will be like trees, branches to branches to more. Then somehow our bonding words will steer into the past, to re-live the sweetness of what has been. We'll talk about November last year, the day we searched for a warm place to spend the evening after the two of us had grown exhausted from the wild gathering of disengaged faces and ruptured conversations. We had decided to go for a walk, didn't we, and soon after, despite the cold that tickled our arms and our ankles, had grown so reluctant to return that we decided to escape to a better place. We discovered a hotel, and we surged straight into the lobby, where we found a table surrounded by a semi-circle of padded seating for the two of us to share. We stayed there for a long time, and we talked, spiritedly, and we shared so many things, but I remember quite specifically, once the ambience had calmed to violins and weightless murmurs, you told me that you knew too well the sensation of feeling unloved, of feeling as though you often tremble only in your own hands. As you spoke I saw your eyes become two sad circles with glints of a splintered innocence, but when you finished sharing that with me, you smiled a smile of unshakable hope, a smile I still remember through every corner. It was there, while we sat with our hands taking turns to encircle the iron teapot, I told you that I met you on three other occasions: once, with the crooked handshake of our nervous dispositions amidst your elated crowd of friends; twice, through the hazy, veil-like curtain where the points of our gazes collided; and thrice, amidst the blooming vanilla orchids under those restless clouds, where the light skips of your feet intersected mine. But that wasn't exactly the truth, for I had met you one other time, on another occasion, before the three I had told you. I'll tell you. It was spring, earlier in the year, and the daffodils and the bluebells and the tulips were coming out together. I had arrived at the garden centre in the slow mist of a morning trance, and that's when I saw you in the corner drawing redcurrants onto a notepad. You moved the pencil on the paper as though you were chiselling away at something of the grandest importance. I'll tell you how focussed you appeared to be, that your face was all screwed up in immense concentration, and I found that endearing and a little humorous and I chuckled to the ground as though I was entertained by the grass. And then I'll tell you that we saw each other for the briefest moment before you returned to your drawing. Then, as the afternoon melts, we'll talk about anything, insignificant as it may be, how a second is to a minute what a year is to six decades, or the changing faces of streets we've grown accustomed to, the polarity between the place they seemed when first encountered and the place they became after time spent with them, just like how over time a room can morph into so many places, each filled with particularly different airs painted by the mood. Ah, the candle, we must not forget, we must put it out before we fall asleep. But not yet, no, not yet. Then we will ponder and we'll laugh together after stumbling into a wall of thoughtlessness because we will have exhausted ourselves just a little. I am attentive to your words, gestures, expressions, and you are attentive to mine and this natural attention will take us here, there and everywhere, and we'll move in synergised motions where time falls under our dominion. Then we will walk over a hill. We'll wave our arms on top of the hill, side to side, and we'll be marvellous, we'll stand like stones draped in feathered wings, and our hair will move like pretty frocks in a violent wind. In the distance we'll see an avid dog chasing a frisbee, and a pale postbox standing alone in the grass, and misty lights clustered at the foothill. We'll follow the lights, and run like it's a race to leave footprints, jumping with the bounce of rubber on solid ground. As we get closer, we'll see the frazzling motions of pedestrians walking over the startling colours of a river's reflection, and from our raised view, they will appear as tiny beings over a spectrum ablaze, like ants dancing on a crystal ball. Then we will sit on a bench and sip on something delicious. We'll discuss something, anything, and then fall into other topics and forget what we were just talking about, again and again. You'll show me songs by Hiroshi Yoshimura, I'll show you songs by Linda Perhacs. You'll point to something in the distance, I'll point to something else. We will be our own perimeter. It will seem as though the sun will fall where we choose to keep it. It will seem as though the wind will follow where we welcome it, that if the dark of the sky should last days it would do so to extend our joy in the conversations of the night. We'll huddle what connects us and keep it tightly packed between us so it never becomes exposed to the world. We'll shove what we have into a jar and then bury it into the sediment of the earth. I would love to cross that meadow with you. I want nothing more than to see what lies on top of that mountain with you. We'll draw a map and point to where our feet should wander, together. We'll build a mansion of magnificent words and discuss the multitudes of life under the shelter of a painted roof. Then we will lay down, just as we are now, and sigh, the sigh in unison after shared merriment. I can feel things fading now. I think now you have fallen asleep. I think that any approaching moment could also take me away. So I will blow out the candle. I will take away this flickering light so we can rest. We are going away now, but it won't be anywhere far and it won't be for long, no it won't, just a little while.

THE SEED THAT BECAME EVERYTHING

The pinewood table lay slightly askew. Through the coating of my eyelashes, sealing with passing seconds, I watched the firm, elegant fingers, along with the contraction of the knuckles, push out the seed through the plump body of the fruit, its roundness becoming disfigured by a fracturing force. My head lay within the cradle of my arms and my eyelids drooped with the weight of exhaustion and a threatening silence, a silence that permeated my foundational sense of being, my base consciousness, a silence that reminded me of being born. I was met with still life, a toneless hum, quiet metallic rings of sound, the whoosh of wind, fleeting illumination like that of passing cars, capricious manoeuvres, loud thumps, distant spoken messages, light phrases, louder phrases, me, you, them, all of us, us in our vacillating, granular existences — then suddenly, out of the blackness and the whiteness of expanding depths, the implosion of new belief, and it was becoming more, and more. Being a part of this motion, this unpredictable sway and ever-growing expansion without a solid sense of myself was not at all a tendency of mine, but it all came swimming through an ocean of emphatic thoughts, outwards and upwards into compartments that hung in the air, shapeless nests of uncountable numbers. The voluptuous laugh ringing in my ears called forth hues of light bursting forth into my sealed vision. The circular stream above my eyes poured inwards, and its descending weight pushed the outlines of distorted terrain straight through the mouths that were murmuring over me, with their wordy phrases and listless movements. And then, out of nothing, we shot out and flew up, breaking through the bounds. Beyond, beyond, beyond we went, into iridescent depths. How spectacular, what a particular ecstasy this was to be cradled in this way, to experience the alacrity of unrestrained potential over the arc of resistance. I was taken to the before, before my prying mind could function with its own mechanism. And now, before me was a brain, my own, the whole of me, a brain that could no longer reach realisations, estimations, seemingly before my own knowledge of time. But upon further integration I realised it wasn't a brain, no it wasn't, it was a seed. Here, I began as a tiny seed, like one of the many scattered dusts frittered in the wind. There was no time within my skin; firmly-coated nothingness was all my small, lifeless body consisted of. Thoughtless, void of emotional capabilities, desires, dreams, I floated between the brink of time and the edge of nothing, far from a home in which to belong, but without an iota of a care to wish for one, with no soul or breathing force beneath my grain of a body, no purpose. But as walls call light to cast projections of shadows, a light had been called to pervade the mass of me. I stood as a gateway for a flare of life, the clasp of a wing of light traversing through transparent depths, light impossible to break, with wisps of flying fragments and stars falling off the break of sudden movements and disseminating into the invisible space through which breath respires, with large, bright sparks of dreams to touch and spread splinters of its unlimited self, again and again. Just as twilight glows with an astral shine, meeting eyes with a distinct touch of purposeful existence, the glowing touch met me. Sudden tiny combustions broke through my outer layer, and then a flint of warmth beckoned from within me, growing from a hint of a slight shimmer to a radiant pulse, shooting out everywhere in light and sonic beams. With the static impulse of exploding stars, I was flown to a vast space, a place where nothing melts, nothing withers, where things only appear and vanish and reappear and multiply and cascade and burst. Rapid imagination, an imagination so profoundly vivid, so tightly tethered to every possibility of becoming — it summoned me, or what I had engendered, which I surmised was something akin to nothing and the fusion of all forms simultaneously. Below me I felt only boundless air, and my vessel, without firmness or shape or reason, assumed a sudden form, a form that positioned me in space and endowed me with a sense of separateness, but it wasn't an insular separateness, rather it was an expansion of a one-self, where there was duality in individuality. A new light had awakened. It found me. And I was given choice, choice to become. Now I was experiencing myself as a thing that contained a beating pulse, a tunnel of passing air — but could I be more? Could I be gifted with the budding grasp of sensation, with the initiation of becoming and becoming more through my own volition? I was no longer a seed, but an arrangement, an expanding arrangement, ever-growing with the kiss of nourishment, a composition of compounds with a forming trajectory of reason, with the acute sense of what it was to desire revealing itself through the pounding thrum that was inside of me, a thrum with the intuition of pursuing, reaching, awakening a new stream of affirmation into an area that could not be held, nor touched. Space had become an extraordinary environment, a single dimension of limitless faces and facets, and I saw, all around, scattered particles that were becoming more, more, more. I saw breath in wandering entities, each moving in this boundless space, fulfilling their own pursuits.

And again I felt the keen sense of becoming, a want to become. Everything at which I looked, I could become. I was a multilayered being shifting in complexities, shaped by the infinite corners of a grand mind. I looked upwards, to the gliding smokes of cloud that were in every shape, then down, to the grains and gradients and materials beneath me. It seemed that life was a fusion of parts, and I was to play my part, and in doing so I could be any part I desired. In the distance I saw roots with the inherent knowledge of creation growing and spreading through the rich moisture of the ground, and I discovered the inherent vastness of me in the way they shot into the air — flying currents awakening into greater scopes in the patterns of time. Further, I saw with an inward sight the bodies of intricate structures. Could I learn their point of angulation, circumference and diameter? I saw the unending fantasies in their contorting shapes and figurations. Could I carve my own aesthetic understanding that could exist outside of myself? I became fused with roving passion that searched along the courses of winding trajectories for a point of actuality, a temporary completion, looking in the spaces between for small specks of discovery that would create expansive activity. What is the relationship between everything around? What is the function of all that I can see? Within every space lay endless rows of information that trailed in writhing spirals between the torrent of phantom-like bodies, linked in the harmony of one, independent in the minds of many. And around me, I heard the brilliant cords of connection. What are these multitudes of communication I do not know? A sonic beam, ornamented with layers of sonorous colour, flew overhead and touched the sphere above, sending off magnetic whirs of colour all around, colour awakened through the welcoming of the encompassing skies. How can I construct a translation of my feelings into this eccentric form? I wanted to become, to know, to learn, to shift into a soaking vessel with the pores of erudition, and then to burst into a resounding drum of insight and articulation. I wanted to hear the rush of those invisible waves of air, and listen to the song of those echoic chambers in the ground, the texture of those pointy clusters of green, the rumble of those creaks in the wind, and feel the force of this warmth that simmers with the influx of scattering particles, and the trace of this trickling, transparent rush, the soak of those round orbs of colour. I wanted to experience the soar of that spurt that falls through open space, the droplet of that syrupy flow of liquid, the grind of those solid and mighty structures, the spark of that spirited connection, and that one, and that one. With this roaring appetite, I was expanding into more, and with the finding of all that I could perceive, the result of it all was the fine understanding that I was, once again, a seed. Just a seed. The opening of my eyelashes allowed light to find my waking awareness again. The seed now lay on the plate. The hand glistened with the juice from the fruit. The pinewood table lay slightly askew.

A TASTE FOR SWEET THINGS

The steps of feet I heard on the large open field with masses of healthy grass all around were not like the usual hurried steps I was used to hearing back home. *What did they sound like?* Well, they were something like gentle caterpillar marches, with rhythmic frivolity, a pitter-patter in skipping strides. Six or seven little drummers, far away but close enough for their bonks and claps to be heard, glistened on the side, and crystalline streaks of sun fell downwards in strings and spirals, lending their light to the maple trees all neatly clustered, scattered where they belong. The bends and twirls of the stone path below me were becoming second nature to each step of mine, and I walked with a slow whimsicality, a little bend of fascination, of passion, in each step. When I arrived at a stop to refill my bottle from an arched stone water fountain, not too far away I saw a girl, with shoulder-length hair, so shiny it almost constructed a reflection. *What colour?* The same dark colour as mine. *As yours?* Yes, as mine. She was standing with her arms and fingers out like flourishing vines, her pose like an ancient statue brought to life. She was by a shrub that yielded heaps of wild berries. I watched her pick them, one swiftly after the other, unearthing hidden pieces of herself with every little tug. She had a wicker basket attached to a shoulder strap of satin or something with a similar sheen across her shoulder. One by one, each berry broke apart and fell into the basket; perhaps a small pile of hundreds of berries were forming in there — I couldn't quite see — but I imagined she'd fill it and take it home, maybe she'd make a jam or the filling of a pie, or let them sit nicely by the window for fingers to pick as they wandered by. I stood there, noticing my infatuation and thought: how had I lived all these years and not once picked freshly ripe berries from the generous stems of a grand shrub? *Is that so?* Yes, and without a flicker of premeditation, my feet led me to it, and I stood beside her, and with an inquisitive pinch in my fingers I plucked a berry and compressed it between my teeth and the tip of my tongue, summoning the living sweet juice and allowing it to become a part of me. How ravishing, tasteful, melodious. All I needed was to step into the occasion, to put forth my arm and grab the opportunity to taste, and in doing so I had inserted myself into a brand new experience. I was basking in a reified pleasure of the world's finest and ever-growing sugar. I had revived a certain taste, a taste for sweet things. *And the girl?* The girl, seemingly engrossed in my elation, turned to me and said something in her native language, and though I didn't understand, I knew that she was communicating to me a bestowal of our shared elation, and as I looked at her I somehow understood through the pulse beneath her words.

What happened next? I boarded a train that journeyed to a rural town among many hills. I was told by a man in linen who served me slices of the purest carambola that there I would find teahouses and street-food shacks and luminescent alleyways, all hidden in a cleft. *A cleft?* Yes, between two mountains. The carriage rumbled and rocked down the evanescent fields of corn and barley, salt fields and salt ponds. I couldn't refrain from pondering on the brink of a reverie when I saw the dusky shadows becoming fractured by the pouring light of a newly blooming day over the lands. It was peaceful, and this compelling calmness stunned me and kept me an inch above the rumbling floor. And when I saw, wrapped in a gentle slice of some apricot-coloured fabric, the small, bobbing head of a green pigeon with beady eyes and an expression of utter fragility, there was a sense in me as I apprehended what was seen, a sense of being born into a new foundation, an arrangement of new and unrestrained variety, far from the system of the unchanging, the tedious, that I had been so accustomed to. I sensed that, in a fleeting gesture, my foresight of predictability had been dispelled and scattered vigorously so I could no longer grasp it, and all I could do was descend into the prospect of all the invisible forms that were approaching and soon to be revealed to me. And it was acutely felt, almost seismic, perhaps perfect.

I arrived, eyes wide as a swan's open wings. Give me more of this. Give me more of this spring of splendour, I thought as I stepped off the train and onto a pathway of minuscule stones, powdery and sporadic underneath my stepping feet, sending off sandy mists with every step. I continued forth. Trees. *Trees?* Trees, alluring and distributed all around like friendly, otherworldly beasts, perched in their silent slumber, and breathing in the breeze. I followed the bend and let it take me to the special place I had been anticipating. I heard distant soothing vibrational bells, or perhaps gongs, amidst the shrill but slight cry of a rubbery squeak and grinding stone that seemed to be not far away. And then an echoic call. It was a voice. *A voice?* It called again. I walked on. And again it called. It was a child. I walked further. It kept on resounding. I stepped over a log. It called again. *What did it sound like?* It was a happy call, an upwards shout of brilliant ecstasy, and it poured in with the sounds of other voices — a kaleidoscope of human chatter, fading in, fading in. And it became louder, but not too vigorous, but rather it played on a faultless level into my ears, melodic as strings and brass, light as woodwind, and ubiquitous as falling snow. I soon approached a bookseller; he stood beside piles and piles of books, books of plentiful shades and colours, distributed on top of each other like rows and columns of brick-like structures, a city of paper architecture. *Then what happened?* Then there were oranges, bountiful and round. They reminded me of the type of oranges I sought to fill the wicker basket I kept on the kitchen counter back at home — plump and filled with juice, deep in colour and round with the curvature of a globe. Further on, I came across a large table, and on it a plethora of hand-painted cabinet knobs, endlessly pretty and aligned in a constellation. I stood by and my hand wandered over. With eyes on them all, together the paint seemed sprinkled with beautifully chaotic disorder, cosmically vibrant and with a message abstruse to a single human gaze. The captured smile behind the table lingered in my short-term memory as I browsed the many circles. I didn't speak her language, nor did she mine, but I attempted to tell her with my hands and my eyes and brows the way I captured the allure of these things. I knew that she, like architects, roof thatchers and butterfly catchers, had eyes for the fine details that exhibit beauty in tiny chinks and specks, that take form as scattered freckles on the many subjects of sight, incredibly easy to miss. And the little manifestations of such a wondrous eye here, stood before me, at the touch of my hands. *So what did you do?* I thought maybe I'd take one for each person that came to mind, and bring them back home and disseminate them to these loved ones. Or I'd keep them for myself, for my home; maybe I'd change all the knobs in my kitchen, or in every room — maybe I'd give every cupboard one of these meticulously detailed little things, then I'd be living in a land of beautiful circles. But no, I was travelling light, I couldn't possibly take all of that with me. I'd take one, I decided, and treasure it like a small being, take it home and find the perfect cupboard in the perfect spot for it to live. It would be the special knob, the odd knob, the knob that would never go unnoticed by neither myself nor anyone that would step foot in my home, the knob to which every guest would point with their mind and question and admire. *But which colour?* Which colour? That's exactly what I was thinking. Which colour would be best suited for this role? My hovering hand became drawn to one, almost instantaneously upon contemplating this. I chose green, a lovely tamed green, to mark the natural element I had fostered within myself to permeate my ideas into my surroundings. Green was the colour. It reminded me of the verdant vegetation I so breezily passed by, falling into fondness that began with a quick glance, but also the sage I had recently grown and grew to adore, and furthermore my grandfather's scarf that, as a child, I watched him use as a celestial partner when he danced in the living room, his movements lit by lamplights that gave their soft glow to the windows and his rolling shoulders catching glimpses of the moon.

I was wandering, long and far through the stone steps with their wonks and charms, around the bends of bamboo pillars, red lanterns, golden flares. A passageway, secretly tucked away and perhaps rarely traversed, called me to make my way down its narrow body and up through the many slants and cracks of unseen adventure, out of site from the roaming eyes below. I saw heads appearing through windows where people sat on cushions and drank tea alongside creaking of wood and tunes of breeze sneaking through crevices, and bows and pillars and the whistles of twin-pipe nose flutes. And at the summit of steps carved onto rooftops, my hands on a parapet,

I felt the gust of a friendly wind. It was the same wind that poured its soul over the many mountains in the misty distance, containing a breadth with no start or end — mystical invisible mayhem. It rushed. My hair blew. My knuckles tightened. *And how did you feel?* I felt anew. This feeling was the unravelling of ropes from aching wrists, it was the revealing of blue in the sky after a day of grey, the blessing of rain after a drought. Memories, heartache, broken attachments, severance, sadness, wounded care — it was all surfacing, and I was letting go. And I believe that I cried, but I wasn't too sure, and if I did, gone were my tears in the instant of a blink, carried, scattered, distributed onto the mountains. Somehow, through the wind, I was saying goodbye to the harmful, the unwanted, the muddy substances I no longer wanted to keep. This was me saying goodbye. This was the work of departure, the art of divorce. And when the wind passed I was left with a cleared mind, with the lightheartedness in the skip of a child's step, and I channelled this in my motions, in the trail of my drifting, journeying thoughts. Soon, I sat on a bench in a garden gated by the ethereal glows of lanterns with tassels hanging beneath their bodies, interconnected by a single undulating string, drawn in the sky as though a dolphin had carried it through its swim. I looked down at the grass, blooming with an inherent sheen, and then to a tree, and then I saw, just beside my shoe, a praying mantis. *A praying mantis?* Yes, a praying mantis that lay on a leaf at the root that trailed to the base of another tree. And then I looked at the specks and agglomerations of tiny spiked flowers scattered in pretty dishevelment. *And what were you thinking?* Living, living and its intricate wonders. I sighed, for I could do nothing else to encapsulate this feeling.

I walked down the footpath that cut left and right in and out of homes like a perplexing labyrinth with no end in sight. But soon I saw lights streaming in through the mouth of the passage, and they were begging me to witness the charming illusions they emitted, and they became vaster and wider and more complex the closer I got to them. *What were they?* I wasn't sure, but they were frazzled and splattered, and moving. *Moving?* Yes, they were swaying almost, round and round. *Round and round?* Yes, round and round and round. Circles and circles, and the circles became fiercer and more vivid the closer I approached. And when I got to them, my eyes beheld a carousel, splendidly lit with the glowing marigold of a falling sun and the swirling rotation of the ocean's ebb tide spilling through the surfaces of the utmost, foremost heart. And there was a twinkling waltz, a melodious companion to the moving spectacle. I was no longer there in a hidden street of a suburban village, I was in a fantasy, a wild fantasy, where seven horses galloped over my head, their multi-layered shadows falling into my hands. The spinning geometric pattern in the steel pole twirled its way to the top where rows and rows of lightbulbs, gold as maple, shone magnificently down onto the white horses, with manes holding the fierceness of the wind. I took a few steps closer. Birds. *Birds?* There were birds. They were sitting on the horses. I squinted my eyes and stepped closer, spellbound. They had tiny blue bodies, tender, opulent and lucent, and strikingly dark navy faces, perhaps even black, with red beaks and these stunning yellow-medallion eyes I could never forget. Then a few of them flew away, out into the sky, and then a handful of others arrived, landing elegantly onto the horses, one after the other. These birds, I pondered, they could soar in the sky at any time they wished, reaching heights beyond any cloud in sight, but yet they chose to be here, sitting, basking on the carousel. *But why?* Perhaps they admired the magical simplicity of being carried by an exterior motion. Perhaps they just wanted to experience the simple drifting movement, tranquil in such a distinct simplicity and caught in the immersion of the honey-glare in the lights and the scintillating music. To do nothing but rest in being and allow the experience of the carousel to happen to them. To let it take them on its own ride, where they could exercise no control and simply be moved in the round and round perpetual motion — circles chasing circles like days following nights. Perhaps they enjoyed this difference, this contrast, this divergent experience. Perhaps they found comfort in it.

What happened next? Then I wandered gently into myself as I discovered in me the pursuit of gaining something from this strange, eccentric sight. My hands know the touch of the wind, they know the touch of glass, of feathers and the movements of endless grains of sand passing along their edges; but unlike my eyes, they do not know the beauty of the sunset, or unlike my mouth and nose, the richness of wine, or the wonderment of harmony that graces my ears. And these birds, I do not know why they chose to sit on these swaying statuesque horses when the unlimited trails of the air were just a flight away, when the reverent wind was their greatest companion, but as I looked at them, into their tiny yellow eyes, following the movement that carried them, somehow I understood them. And maybe it was as simple as that. When I stared into these birds, it seemed after a little while that I'd flown into their core, and somehow my sense of me became fully intact, but all the while almost disintegrated, combusted by the power of these glowing orb-like movements. And so I was consumed. We were so close, these birds and I, infinitely merged. This is the great generosity of design, I thought with my eyes wide open, the point in the needle of becoming, the vivacity of light, the potent breath that guides the shape-shifting swirls in the murmuration of starlings. And it's here, in a glimpse in the space between my temples. It's here. *It's here?* It's here.

POMEGRANATE

I am heading down the spiralling channels of narrow spaces, sunlight coming into view through little ring-shaped spectacles, hitting the surfaces. On the side I notice a seagull hovering fancifully in mid-air. Now a crow steals the spotlight, its stature tenebrous and sharp-like, and it sits, waiting, as though it's prying on the daylight. A pointed pagoda, prominently red, sticks out of the tree tops from afar, a finger to the sky, a pin-prick to the infinite blue; the troposphere has been pierced, and through the tiny hole, a splinter of cosmic insight squeezes through and comes to meet the ground. Through the curve in the corner of the newspaper on the bus, I glimpse heartfelt words. Lovers, siblings, friends? I am not quite sure. But those details don't matter. Hands move gently, like those of harpists. Eyebrows crease in gentle, sympathetic motions. There is a kind of release there, an emancipation of understanding. Words are snatched in the cacophony of trees against the windows, but a glistening body in every syllable pierces through the noise and permeates the enclosed air around us. When the sun sets, I run along the road that borders the great woods. Looking at these trees, I wonder in a momentary mist, my gaze feverish with dreaminess. Each tree stands so differently, but together they are almost one. Each tree holds the hands of its wild neighbours, locked into a silent ritual in a language only they are capable of speaking. Sycamore to my left, you are just like every sycamore tree I've seen and you are also nothing like anything I've ever seen. Cedar to my right, look at you, victim to impermanence, but nevertheless, master of your own individuality. There is a building passing me by; it is wrapped in climbing leaves. I'm enchanted by buildings with climbing leaves around them, the way they grow and sprout, encompassing the structure of the walls. The ivy, the honeysuckle, the clematis — I notice the movements they have travelled, slow and incomprehensible, lively and unpredictable. I close my eyes and there's a room through the corridor of my imagination, a room in which I am sitting on a chair of wonderful oak, a chair submerged in the foliage of vines and leaves, spreading out, seeking formation and shooting along the surfaces like train tracks, working together, never once overlapping. In front, there is a wall with paintings and photographs in ornate frames through which the vines travel. Somehow they know just where to go to construct a splendid picture. Before me is a grand piano, rough and worn but in some perplexing way more glamorous than any piano I have ever seen. The vines wrap around the pedals, travel along the legs, and across the lid. The keys are left untouched, as though the plants refuse to obstruct the melody of the song that is playing. And the song dances and leaps through wild and brilliant gushes; its richness is untouchable and its perfection strikes my heart with an invisible arrow, but then I discover it is not an arrow, it is a connective vine from which more vines grow. I notice this when I feel the flutter of the leaves and I look down to see that I have been penetrated, pierced by an ever-expanding curiosity. Now they move through me too. Now I too am a part of these vines that grow outwards and outwards, I am an essential piece in their journey; I provide them with a vessel from which to expand, a temple to grow new avenues. And these vines, continuously moving in harmony, unceasingly seeking exploration and all that is new, they sprout and they pulse, they hook and they weave, they wrap and they spread, they seek and they discover, expanding their understanding through me and us all.

Now, on this patch of grass that shoots up from the ground in gentle spikes, we spin and twirl like the earth. In fact, we all spin together, the earth and us, side by side, and this is how it is, eternally. Much like an unclouded decision that briskly proceeds, we move hand in hand, and much like the back and forth of a pendulum, we sway; and I've never felt this sway, this music, this thunderous heartbeat that's joined the small force of mine. And I know I will create a new sway of my own soon, but for now, I'll glide in this torrential downpour of ideas through the rising of blades of grass until one strikes me with enough vigour to alight a chain of events. For now, I'll sail through colours, and oh, these colours, how large their existence is, how individually solid they stand in the webbing of them all. The yellow hint in the eye that caresses the nape of a neck, or the glimmer of light on the edge of a beige shoulder in the summertime, the light that, in unknowable ways, reminds one of the startling glint of the sun on the silver bell of their first bike, that purple bike with clanky training wheels that squeaked with every turn in the road. The red in the crease of the lip that forms with a smile of laughter at the intertwining of hearts that are overjoyed, or the sepia in the sky that is met with gasps and cheers from happy admirers, with their bronze hands that point upwards with the swift ferocity of dolphins jumping out to greet the violet sky above the chorus of a deep blue orchestra. The brown fabric of the sleeve at the base of the excitable hand that reaches for an orange inside the many-hued bowl in the reflection of the mirror, the same mirror that reflects the cream and the forest green of the woven tapestry that was hung with good intentions. These are the colours I search for. These are the colours I have known, and will know as long as time holds me in its sphere of plentiful sights. I feel as though my eyes can embrace for eternity, until they cry, until they are filled with tears. At times tears swell, they shoot out in drips from my eyes and fall into the atmosphere, and into my ears, and sometimes they fall onto floorboards, knuckles, the wind. What substance have my tears not yet touched? I wonder. I wonder how it is so that the tears from others call for my own to fall, how it is so that through the tears of others, I find tapered avenues that lead me to a lens of enhanced sight, where the design of a bountiful world simmers beneath me, and at times engulfs me. And now I've come to understand that tears, in their wet, physical form, are an incentive to keep creating things, to pass on moving messages, to let heat escape aching veins, to mould enchantment into new existences.

Today I am trying to see with brighter, bigger, rounder eyes that pierce through appearances, around the edges of this world of patterns. I find a penny underneath a sad pile of dust beneath the mantelpiece, but when I wash away the specks and brush its surface with the tiny bristles of a paintbrush, instead of finding a small but impressionable answer in the glare of the reflection, I find nothing but the faint outline of my eye with its pearly pupil — it is an eye on vigil, searching for misplaced passion. Then I wash the dirt of the day from the soles of my feet to feel anew, and momentarily, I feel some sort of fade of beginning, but when nightfall dives head first into darkness which soon brings morning, the soil of my temperament, along which anxieties and concerns are spilling, possesses me to treat it, to nurture it so it can be refined once more. So, I let light fall where it falls and do not argue with time, I let the sun beam behind clouds without begging for the consolation of light, I hum the trails of songs that linger in my substratum. Later, I sit in the garden and remember the morning before. It was in the morning before that I met a song, a song that wished, through its delicacy and its touching grandeur, to prompt tears to flee from my eyes. It reached me softly with a loving melody, a stark tune, redolent of things before, touching words in sad articulation, meeting me here like old friends of mine within previous moments in time. The song came over me and submerged me, and inside of it I witnessed memories, like silent prances of the past, lurching towards me through rings and hums. And now that I hear it in the captured memory of yesterday, I wonder if maybe it is more than just a recollection, if maybe it is something deeper, finer, like pinching two fingers on the emotional thread of a cardigan I used to wear, but instead I'm pulling on the strings of time, strings dangled to me as they dance in mid-air to the music, or perhaps they are hovering and it is I who floats to them, lifted by the gathering of harmony, the limitless confounding of a ballad, a song tied to a picture-like memory by a ribbon of melody. And when I play the song once more, moved by the impulse to remember the feeling, fleetingly, it wraps me again, it laces me and lifts me up to the cadenza, wishing to return.

Night arrives, and soon the moon gestures its life-force down to where I stand. I look to it for distraction, or inspiration, or both. The life of the moon? The coincidence of the moon? I don't want to be someone who sits there, bleakly, looks up to it and sees nothing but a white empty ball, glowing pointlessly but in some way sardonically as though it's teasing the fact that it knows life's true purpose and we don't, the fact that it lives through and way beyond our fickle mortality. But sometimes I am that person and I can't help but see it that way. Yet, on a night like this, when I am not, on these days when the spirit of some exterior life force gently taps the edge of my breath, or so it seems, I see the moon as if I know it, but it is not just an it, nor is it a he or a she or a they or anything like it; it simply is, and in that it is all of those things. And I feel that I know the moon, in the same way that I know it is nightfall, and in the same way that I recognise the sound from crickets between the distant grasses, and all the while it knows me too, and in that transient merging of knowing, that symbiotic understanding that words lack the colour to paint, I need to know nothing more.

Soon I hear the call of birds, and I'm reminded of their flight, of their dazzling nature to be splendid beings to which we can look up and remember the flight of our own lives. Birds are persuaded by morning to sing. Clocks are persuaded by gravity to tick. Water is persuaded by light to glisten. It feels as if it's a force, an inscrutable force that swarms everything that lives, and like flowing water, it keeps on and on, it constantly ceases not to be. You can cut water with the finest pair of scissors but it will always flow, it will always keep on giving. I must remind myself that, at times, when I steer away from this water, and cannot easily find a connection to it, it is in these moments that I cultivate a greater knowledge of it, so when I return I am not just aware that I have returned, but of the returning itself, the journey between the two counterparts. I must sometimes fall out of it in order to fall back, and it is in that falling back, in that thrilling contrast of novelty, where new ropes to vaster lands are thrown down to me from the skies. Just like in the deep gut of that night, that night I stumbled into a dream that had no corners to constrain its purpose, a dream made of echoes and nightly signs, and when I awoke my feet sprung to touch the ground before my eyelids fully opened. At first I was dreaming about sudden irregularities, like a triangle abruptly assuming the shape of a square before it decides to morph into a circle, and then quickly breaking itself into smaller circles and disseminating its pieces, losing them in the monstrosity of vast space. Then, suddenly, something changed, the partitions aligned, and I was on the stage, a grand theatre, with the sweeping snakes of underworld currents below the floorboards, chords and bells and mimers waltzing around like seahorses in a current, the filmic lights cascading down, and the ease of a passing migraine that had formed above my shifting eyes due to the trepidation that began in my knees. I looked up as I forgot the pain, and beautiful, beautiful beings watched me, and though I could not see them physically, I felt the echoes of their illuminating smiles. I walked a single step out of the lights, and suddenly I became blinded by speckles of crystal-like substances and frantic glowing spheres dispersing from the chandelier above, harshly vivid lightning bolts. But it felt like utopia, oh yes, it felt like heaven, if heaven was a feeling. After the sun-lit ceiling revealed itself to me through blinking eyelashes and my eyes opened and became round once more, I went to look inside the fridge and the sight of untouched pomegranate in the cold light called me to taste, and so I tasted the pomegranate, spoonfuls and spoonfuls, each little jewel booming like flowerbeds in a garden, bearing a cold, syrupy touch. So fine is every second, so rich, profound. Sweetness such as this, it can only create more, it can only play its role in contributing to the sweetness that surrounds the air, the sweetness that is always here. The world is like a pomegranate — if we get past the firm, tasteless surface, we find all of its good stuff, the seeds of the world, with sweetness in every gap and crevice. And I find thinking in this way intrinsically sweet in and of itself. I enjoy the ripple effect it has. I find comfort in the space of it. Can I be here for a long while? Can I muse on this particular subject with this lens until it coaxes me into a blissful slumber, and then I can sleepwalk my way through life, like this, always? I look outside the window. Here is a fire, a buzz, a concoction, a light. World, alight the depth of my chest with your penetrating rays until it bursts into particles of some unfathomable love, just like this pomegranate falling down into me, and from then on I will share it with whoever wishes to grasp it. I want to share. But first I always need to find. I want to become accustomed to the shadow of a bird's flight, to the lull of midnight wind, to the taste of fresh river.

Tonight, there are elephants here, large and overpowering, each one representing someone that I've known and resisted letting go of, including previous forms of myself. So now their presence is marked forcibly on my visceral awareness, and I can't sleep it off, no, I cannot drift from this, or march away. I must face these elephants, I must make them know where I stand and then allow them to pass me by, without startling them or demanding too much from them. There's plenty of room here, but not quite enough, and not quite enough shelter to guard them all from the grating storm that lies ahead, from the thick downpour of hail stones that the sky delivers in great swooping reminders that time awaits. I must make my move. Once in a while I cannot help but become suspicious of existence, and my eyes meander in trails to find the substance of what is happening, but then I get lost — distraction occurs or inspiration hits — and I find myself living again. At times I think of you, whatever you may be.

But I know you, for I know what lies behind you. You are the thing that keeps me on the ground when I wish to be lifted. You are the thought that arrives after forgotten moments to dim the light I cast to see what lies before me. But why do I still sometimes give you sustenance to be? How do we live so strictly by such absurd fantasies? And why? I'm aware that these things are marked deeply into us in memories as early as childhood play, but surely they cannot touch the deepest part of us, the part of us from where our truest thoughts are summoned. Oh, you. I want to dissect every single thought inside your imaginary little brain and expand them into worlds of their own so I can dive deep into them and extinguish the poison and excavate the essence from each one. You, hand me your melancholia, the bristles of your sadness, and I shall hold it all within me, transform it into an elixir on my heart's furnace, and give it back to you. And I want to tell you that, oh yes, it's possible, that I can mould this mayhem into something with a heartbeat, for me, and for you too. You with your large, solid teeth, bit into my earth, shredded my soil to pieces, and disassembled the young roots of my tree. Now I lay here, seedless and bare, but patient, waiting for a sweet piece of life to fall into me so I can share its heart and create something magnificent.

WHERE IS IT?

I didn't find it in the wind, when it came from inside of that hungry storm and I watched it through the window, sedated in contentment, reminded of the unbounded command of the unseen. I didn't find it in the middle C, or the higher E, or the harmony of their correlation that sprung forth to me. I didn't find it in the motion in the skies when I stayed out to watch the birds arrive and depart, nor did I find it in the sways and swirls of the water by the bank as I brooded and dreamed of being a thin line of light dancing on the glaze. It wasn't in the dainty way my mother greeted me after my first day of school, my tie clotted and hanging off my shoulder like a limp animal, nor was it in the stroke of her palms as she tucked me under the sheets whilst I dreaded returning at dawn. I didn't find it in a single one of those papers, handed to me from sticky fingers belonging to tired minds that knew more about life than I did. I didn't find it in any of those songs my grandfather played to me, pouring out through the karaoke machine, a hollow reverberation surrounding my head like a pulsating bubble of fluid sound, nor did I find it in the silence between them, as I circled the titles in the catalogue with the bright keenness of a pigeons beak. It wasn't in the sound of the siren, the one that flung my shoulders to my ears and swept me under the table as I imagined the room succumbing to a violent shake, nor was it in the vivid tone of the colours on the jewel of the ring I saw beneath the steel gate of the sewers. It wasn't in the rush in my thighs amidst the turbulence of a trembling aeroplane, or the peculiar kerosene smell through the slit in the car window, or the glint on the sharp canine erected by a snarl of a stray dog in the Thai suburbs. I didn't find it hidden beneath any of the coins I collected, pounds and pennies and everything in between, shiny and matt, round and pointed, piled in rows in order of wideness on the windowsill. It wasn't in the mimicry of the moth that I watched through broken binoculars on the glove of a loud educator without a face, or the zest in the juice of the lemon smeared upon the fresh wound beneath my fingernail. It wasn't in the hug that released imprisoned tears and sent qualms fluttering away after frightful hours. It wasn't in the dizziness that subdued me like a spell after the spinning ride at the spring carnival, or in the awe that lingered on my retina at the first sight of a shooting star, speedy and angular like a harmless spike in the sky, sudden as new life. I didn't find it in the solicitude of the friend that lifted me from bloody knees on concrete to the nurture under the shade of a willow tree, nor did I find it in the strike that fell across my cheek through the force of a teacher with a wild temper. I didn't find it in the delirium of frenetic neighbours, the loneliness of priests, the enthusiasm of hearts that never aged. I didn't find it in the formation of stories born out of a black tunnel that grew into a well with adoring waters, or in the bend of a broken finger that stunned me with the strike of an electric hammer, or in the making and the breaking of friendships that came and went, waving goodbye with wild sweeps of celebration and devastation. It wasn't in the weeping shadows ambling through winter, whose unheard prayers became sentiments for better lives, nor was it in the moonlit wishes borne from the charms of happy strangers. It wasn't in the disappointment of missing out on shared whims of childhood play, when I was left with nothing but a splinter and a chipped button from old corduroys, nor was it in the joy in the dance of arms and legs slicing through layers of beacons of light, shooting out pulses of a timeless love. It wasn't in the timbre of my young, teetering voice when I sang countless lyrics to nameless songs and spat through tiny holes of a microphone, unaware of my surrender. It wasn't in the seed of the apricot I examined in sunlight, veined with knowledge and life, its character curved and bristly on the tip of my finger. It wasn't in the rectangular mirror when I smeared mud and grass over my chin and brows, or the circular one when, through my squinting eyelids, I watched ink run alongside rippling water and humorous regret, or the triangular one, through which I saw prisms of light refracting from the surface, purple and pink and blue. I didn't find it in the cloud-filled sky, as I lay on a meadow and felt that I was nothing but a conscious speck sheltered by a dome with a paper-white glare, untroubled and endlessly wide. I didn't find it in the turn of the key as I unlocked the door to a home of new belonging, or in the weight of a tender torso with warm intentions. It wasn't in the curve of the summit on a sunrise-kissed hill, or in the aftertaste of mulled wine, the chimes of French bells, the rumble of unfettered laughter, or in the soaking of brilliant ideas kept between the time-stained pages of 20th-century geniuses. It wasn't in the visceral deluge of the orchestra that convinced the beats of my heart that they were known, that they were understood, or the breath of the world I found breathing me in the frozen second of each present moment.

But, when I sat down by a river, the brilliant arcs and thrums of the invisible air projecting each story on my own empty but colourful vista, and I began to think of all the things I could recall that gave rise to the pursuit of an immortal sediment, beneath the foremost layer of a fragile purpose, and one that I could not find, I whispered a question: "Where is it?"

And, upon finding solace behind my eyelids and vanishing into silent, unmoving wonders, where this vast new area held timeless blends of sights conjured from a mind untethered to forms of thought, I found that the very mould of my question had somehow evaporated, the way fear leaves the body of the swallow whose impulse leads it to swoop in the air, the way a baby's curiosity towards the texture of grass escapes as it strokes its gentle blades for the first time. Then I was called to more questions, questions I asked with a primed engine underneath the shape of each word. What is it about the glow of the moon that calls for wolves to howl, that implores oceans to heave, seekers to gaze? What is it about us wandering particles of change that calls us to sink into the swells of our beautiful and bitter moments? Before me, I watched the river flow, the way it drifted and wandered as if letting go, and within it I saw the life that sends the leaves falling, the life that imparts a shape to each cloud, that sends a bee to a crop, a painter to the colour blue, that lends sadness the sweetness of tears, that gives each moment a mark of silence, heals a wound, causes an organism to grow.

And, I think, perhaps the river told me that to yearn to know is to try to mend an eternally broken fantasy, and one that it wishes never to hold. And to let go is to find, and to find is to be, but not know.

THE LEVITATION OF DOVES

We didn't believe in anything we could not see. And we could not dispose of these thoughts, they only grew more and more, catapulted through the nerves of our widening brains with every new movement in the hollow space between those towering walls, all four of them enclosing the broken whispers of worlds that could never penetrate the plaster clumped together to keep us locked inside, with the thickness of stifled empathy and tenacious demands. We were small, we were mindless and inexperienced, and therefore we had to sit, just sit, clumped together, until those aggravating electric needles along the bends of our legs forced us to move, but even when this occurred, we still had to remain seated, still and sensible as punished mice, for it was not yet time to stand. White clocks, with every single one of their desperately throbbing seconds, had been placed on the top of each wall, just within the line of our central vision, so we could be reminded wherever we looked just how many seconds there were left to endure before we could at last get away and then prepare to do this all over again. Back in class, we sat with hands on the tables — a pencil, a rubber and a ruler aligned symmetrically in the corner if you were a notable student — and never our elbows, no, never our elbows, for that would only lead to the temptation of dumping our chins in our hands, and what a terrible sight it would be to appear so languid, or worse, indifferent, oh no, instead it was expected that our eyebrows raise at every line to which that steel pointer points, that our feet never fidget, and we must converse enthusiastically at the gateway of every new conversation topic, we must raise our arms up high if we have an appropriate question, but most importantly, we must never need to use the bathroom unless our bladders absolutely implore us to, and in this unfortunate case it is our wrongdoing for filling them before stepping into the room. This all came about through the sharp directions of those two conspirers in dark draping materials who told us so, who stipulated with monotonic lethargy and mouths that drooled for sustained order that this was the way things must be, always. They were both tall, floating above us all with their superiority and arcane knowledge that consisted of a supposed firm hold on the steering wheel of living and a repertoire of long words that we weren't even certain our parents knew. Through a surreptitious sidewards glance between the ringing of bells, I occasionally saw them whisper mumbles of fractured sentences to each other in the corridor as they hovered discreetly to their meeting room that had blinds obscuring the windows at all times. There wasn't a second of the day when those blinds were raised; they may as well plaster planks of wood against those illusory windows, or have no windows at all, just solid walls, I sometimes thought. In the room covered with papers of splatted colour and paper mâché and overused hairdryers that were used to quicken the drying of paint, I stood by the wall. It was a green wall, a distinct olive green, and the little broken bumps and dots of stains made it a wall that was unlike any other wall; it was a remarkable display, a formation that could only partially be understood by the rare few who studied its secret complexities. The art teacher, with her sumptuous tendrils of hair and her fluttering garments through which she majestically moved, was one of the few who never looked with dismaying eyes, who never spoke poorly about eccentricity and caprice, never scolded the happenings of what lay outside of the rulebook. This classroom was a special place, concealed in the top corner of the building, a place where things were possible and no longer stilted mysteries, a place where, once walked through the door, one could unravel every layer of themselves without the hostility of unemotional giants in blazers and buttoned shirts that the lot of us were so accustomed to. The art teacher had a gaze that steered forwards rather than downwards, so when she would look at us, despite our collective smallness, it was almost as though she would lift us to her elevated place. I felt this; it made me feel that I could somehow be known here, that I could be heard, and my ideas could become more than shy words. Now I want to be like this wall, I thought whilst I stood up against it, my arms melting into the colour and propelling upwards, downwards, upwards again, the many little scabs of dried paint gently scratching across my hands, delicate constellations moving finely through and between my fingers. I enjoyed this sensation, and when I tilted my head back just a bit and met, up close, the intimate nature of this wall, it was only a matter of seconds before I understood the colour, the patterns, the character, before I felt that I too was made of the very same components, that transiently I had morphed into an embodiment of these undiscovered aspects of something so repeatedly overlooked, that I too was the green wall. The green wall was the place to be. The green wall was the place to become anything. I was certain that I had not yet seen anyone play the guitar in front of my eyes before, not until I encountered the girl with the checkered ribbon dangling from her hair. It was during class hours and the playground through the window seemed as though it were a forbidden wilderness, a place far beyond the bounds of where

I could step foot, and this hair-raising serenity would remain until the sound of that commanding bell, then somehow its invisible gates would open and it would invite the quakes and swells of the exterior world again into its half-hushed heart. And it was so still; I almost felt that I was standing within the borders of a photograph, captured in the hidden bliss of a single frame. I had been given the golden opportunity to deliver the class register to the front reception, and it was during my way back to class, as I breathed in the abundant scent of empty hallways, that I caught sight of the playground, deserted, stepped on by not a single foot. I knew it was prohibited territory, and I didn't even need to try to imagine the shrill sound of the call that might pierce through me if I were to be seen, a call that would shake me immediately out of my adventurous state. But a little pervasive force that began in the tip of my fingers as they fantasised about turning the doorknob, that whispered to me that the risk was worth the experience before I could even pause and question my instinct, kicked in with a quivering impetus. I stepped out, and immediately I noticed that the air felt different — there were no howling yells to absorb the touch of it, there wasn't a single wave in a crowd of maroon jumpers to hinder the force of it, there was no activity I had set my eyes on to take my attention from it. The air was just like the air beyond the gates that encircled this entire place; it had come here with the same ever-changing pleasant spirals that I had felt everywhere *but* here; it had squeezed through the tight gap of a sealed law; it had reached beyond its bounds just like I had; it knew of my rebellion and wished to share a slice of this mutinous rush with me. I walked some steps forward and then round the edge of the brick wall, and that's when I saw the girl with the checkered ribbon. She was sitting casually on a bench, strumming some chords on an auburn acoustic guitar. I was sure that she had never seen or heard of me, and though we had never spoken, I had known of her. Her father was the music teacher — hence the musical instrument liberties — and that was something everybody knew but for some reason we all consciously tried to forget. Now she looked at me too, and as I continued to walk with awkward footsteps that landed with staggers of uncertainty, it was evident that we were going to interact, for it was just the two of us in this wide space that appeared wider and wider and more excitingly and excruciatingly off-limits the further on I walked. An inviting carton of pineapple juice sat beside her. She continued moving her hands along the strings as I approached her, appearing unbothered while simultaneously bewitched by the two or three chords uttered through her unyielding hands. She questioned my venture and I enjoyed the sound of her voice. Being mindful of the connection to her father, I told her I was feeling ill and that my teacher said I could step outside for some air. She told me she had scraped her knee terribly during lunch break and the sight of her bloody wound began making her feel queasy, so the school nurse had allowed her too to get some air. She asked if I wanted to see the wound and I said yes and she proceeded to unstick the edge of a pastel plaster and reveal a red, wet patch of flesh oozing with glimmering bodily juices. She said it looked a lot worse before. I thought it looked bad as it was. We didn't talk much from then on — if we did it would have been only trivial remarks — but somehow we quickly found a bond in those sweet variations of chords and notes, the low notes, the high notes, the ones betwixt the lows and the highs, faintly running around the developing hem of our sprightly ears. Afterwards, she said she wanted to show me something, so I tentatively followed her into the far corner of the playground to a spot where a log lay on a disorderly patch of grass. Then she lifted the log — I had never seen anyone do that — and underneath revealed a stormy horde of trailing insects and invertebrates. Ants, centipedes, millipedes, woodlice, stacks and stacks of them crawled around, the sight of them collectively fuzzy and disorienting. The ceiling of their intimate dungeon had been grimly ripped off and their silent home had become exposed to the unfaltering winds and unpalatable light rays. And this new checkered-ribbon friend of mine, she adored them, for she was grinning and laughing with a farcical sprout. I asked to borrow the guitar, and as she admired the congregation of those tiny dark speckles moving beneath us, I gently plucked the strings. One, two, three, the notes delicately rolled forth, and as my eyes followed those minuscule footsteps trodding through the moist granules of dirt, I wondered if these little things could perceive the sound of music, if they could recognise a distinction between each note, or if they lacked the wherewithal to reach such estimations. And I played for them, and us, for all of us. And then came the weekend, the two precious days squeezed between the tip and the tail of drawled coercion — once Friday had arrived it always seemed to come sweeping through just like that. Just like that it was the weekend, again at last. Again. Perhaps that is the perfect word that pertains to the way I felt about it. Again. I always wanted the weekend. Again and again. The weekend was the time in which I would know of *no* time, and I'd persistently tumble into its measureless embrace; if it was time to feed the cat, or if it was the time my favourite cartoon was airing, or if it was time for my uncompromising after-dinner snack — toast with butter and jam and a milky tea — which tended to be between eight and eight thirty, then I would fleetingly become aware of the time, but it was only a matter of minutes before I'd flutter into the deep-set clouds of no time, no time at all, nothing but here and there and this and that and me and you and us. One weekend, I was gifted five notes of five pounds, clean, unscathed and for only me. We were visiting my aunt who lived in Brighton. I remember she took me down to the pier, and that's where she placed those abundant sheets of paper into my palm, pressing my fingers down over them tightly. I was given the freedom to spend this money on whatever I pleased, and so I pranced into the arcade, and after I had exhausted myself there I purchased a waffle and a tub of bubbles and a laser pen and some stickers. Then we were on the beach. The offing was tinted with a whisper of purple; the spume of the waves foamed and fizzed like miniature avalanches, spluttering curiosity everywhere; the stones and pebbles shone with wetness and moonlight, inviting speculative fingers to touch their suave, bodiless souls, splendidly smooth. I went up to the salty waters. My aunt was waiting far back from me. Kneeling by the white tips ebbing to my squeaking rubber shoes, I felt inside of my pocket and pulled out the very last five-pound note. With my two hands, I bent, creased and contorted the note into a wonky caricature of a boat, faintly recalling from a faded compartment in my mind the distant memory of the origami scene I had watched in a film, the precise moment I put my eyes on every single pixel and rewinded the frames again and again vociferously until I could emulate the elusive system of the hands. And here I had it, my little boat of white and turquoise. I placed it onto the hand of a wave as if it were an infant boat and I were sending it off to play in the shoreline of the humungous depth through which it would one day roam. I watched it be handled and hauled by the wave, and then another, and another, its journey ending a small number of feet in front of me as it toppled over and vanished. I remember it vanishing; it was so sudden that I forgot about it quite suddenly too. I enjoyed the contrast of being there. What a tranquil little town Brighton was; it was nothing like London. Oh, London. The eclectic city, in my eyes, was a shattered pandemonium bursting with crowds and swarms of thunderous dimensions, a place where one could see both beauty and ugliness from any angle, where one would find surprises at even the calmest hour of the day, where cries and laughter and murmuring words and chasing cars and harrowing labyrinths and nervous impulses and fake smiles and long-awaited hugs and horns and hisses lay within every crevice, down every alleyway and every cul-de-sac. Under a single flair of sunlight that pierced through the fluff of a cloud and my sullen temperament, I saw three ringneck doves perched upon the head and each shoulder of a hunched-over seed thrower by the oceanic pond of a park we often visited on the weekends. Doves were not often seen here, so this moment was a treat. Startlingly quick, the person hoisted a handful of seeds up into the air, and all three doves, with resplendent elongation of the wings, hovered upwards to catch the seeds. Their instinct for flight knew the secret of no restraint; their divulged grace understood the circumference of the split-second of the moment; their lightning reaction could taste the very nucleus of each seed merely at the summoning of the rising image of them against the pale clouds. But it was their journey into the air that caused my eyes to lock onto such an effortless levitation. Those three doves held the key to the sky, and I had never *truly* witnessed a bird fly until this instant. I had found a state of belonging, and it was in the levitation of doves. The metallic reverberation of trains through railways and tunnels was a sound I knew as well as my own. I had felt the heave and heard the squawky weep enough times to predict those clamorous inflections. But I enjoyed it all; I found comfort in watching the tunnel lights pass by like bats with lanterns hanging from their fangs; I liked the diversity of appearance on each carriage, the fact that it was always new, the fact that every ride was nothing like the others before. It must have been a late Sunday afternoon and we must have been going home from something rather exciting because I remember the pang of realising my time to roam was running low, and I began holding onto the sensation of everything that was here and now so I could sustain these vanishing instances. A cluster of people huddled together by the doors caught my attention. There were four of them. They wore layers and fine details of character and colours with patterns I had only ever seen on materials draped over the counter of markets with thoughtfully handmade textiles and artefacts. And they were laughing, each one of them, together, in an open but mystically shielded place they had created through the meeting points of their wide-eyed attentions. I studied their connection, the ardent smiles, making vague sense of what was happening on an unseen level, the interconnected stream of minds that formed the outline of an assembled whole, an amorphous world they had erected, impenetrable. Listening to the spark of their bond, I couldn't help but smile all the way home. Oh, the weekdays had yet again arrived. And that was exactly how I felt about it, the thunderous clap of a monosyllabic remark — oh. The canteen was a vibrant area. It was a hall of chirping fledglings, loud and monstrous acts, and the silly tottering gossip of our young wits over sandwiches and fruit juice, a place where we could unite our elbows and tangle our opinions over bento trays. I would occasionally fall into moments in which I'd lose focus of the conversation taking place over the table and subsequently become swarmed in the frenzy of a million mouths all talking at once. In these moments, I'd often place my fingers in the doors of my ear canals and jitter them in and out quickly. The result was a turbulent tremolo, and when I closed my eyes and did this the sound morphed into an expanding pattern of wild rows of tendrils that surfaced the line of great immensity. It was a grey day outside the windows, the day I was struck with a fever and a swarming case of disorientation in the teeming canteen. I remember standing up halfway through my meal and looking all around. I could see it all, wrapped in a sequence of immensely hyperreal flashes. I saw everything. Stain-smeared cutlery, mashed potatoes with yellow patches, smouldering custard, wrinkled plastic, gleaming polished wood, white flakes between clumps of greasy hair, estranged crust of brown bread, almonds and oranges, more oranges, oranges with too much pith, pith and pith and pith, eerily thick apple juice, blackcurrant and raspberry juice, drips of indistinguishable juice in the crease of a dimple, tears falling from a tantrum, milk dripping from a chin, consolatory palms, gravy, sponge cake, gravy, sliced figs, gravy, sickly brown gravy that made my belly wreathe, murky water, limpid water, scabrous knuckles, remnants of bathroom soap, soil-stained clavicles, braces, oddly sharp canines, sweaty necks, eroded exercise books, concealed tamagotchis, hair clips, noses, white walls, dinner ladies, mounds of soft broccoli, candy bracelets, freshly snipped fingernails, stringed cheese, marshmallow chocolate, butter, jam, salted flaky crackers, eye rolls, donut holes, wobbling thighs, ear lobes, grapes, soggy crumble, soft nods, clapping hands, scones, fidgeting fingers, ravelled fingers, finger-poked cotton holes, peanut butter, raised shoulders, trenchant remarks, people, people, people and all that they contain in the tightly organised compartment of a hollow chamber. I had to force out several tears in the medical room before I could be relieved by the succumbing nod of the nurse which meant I could go home early. Who knew being ill could bring so much elation? It was thrilling to be leaving at lunchtime, beautiful and seemingly illegal. In the car on the way home, I was seeing the world through the window at a forbidden hour, and despite my fever, it was a satisfying time. But soon I was to return. I was always to return whether I liked it or not, and I had accepted this protocol — I had to. But I must add, this place wasn't all morning gloom and dreary afternoons as my words may portray, no, I often found myself smiling at the discovery of new things, at the gleeful sharing of ideas among the fascinated ones, at the amusing illustrations on the board, the lavish piano in the music room, the cosiness of cold mornings, the rhythmical way the numeracy teacher explained fractions, the extracurricular activities like the short-lived clarinet lessons I partook in before I realised they were taking away my precious time beyond the gates. And I had friends, two close ones and a large bunch of outer-circle playmates. The games we played seemed to come out of infinite concepts and expansive collaboration; at times I wished they'd never end. We would chase each other, and we'd pretend, lose ourselves in the land of make-believe, we'd steal chalk from the teacher's cupboard and covertly draw on the playground bricks and concrete corners, knowing soon the rain would wash our secret messages away, we'd scramble across the hallways, we'd talk in our own playful languages that occasionally boarded the realm of gibberish. Vast imagination was almost always accessible when we were together. The changing room was a stifling place. It was there that I encountered harsh words, foul remarks, kids imitating cruelness. It mostly came from a particular small group of boys; they happened to be the ones who were admired by many for running the fastest and kicking the balls the strongest. As we waited for the teacher to return and assign us into running groups, one of them placed his hand on my shoulder and made a sound that suggested approval and acceptance. They admired me because of a lucky last-second point at basketball I had scored, and on this occasion they seemed to have hand-picked me as one of the few who had earned their respect, honouring me with an unspoken token that gave me a pass on the mockery and the teasing. Their esteemed combination of forces had a startling power over everybody else. They were revered, but by an odd, pressured exertion, intimidation masquerading as admiration. They were celebrated for their impressive abilities in the field, making them heroes of playground accolades, and they were always watched, their ability to possess the spotlight was unprecedented in my eyes. But they could be mean, they were unceasingly begging one another for approval and attention by hammering down their hidden fragility on others, throwing down pieces of their own troubles as empty stones of words on the soft spots of those they deemed to be beneath them. And they were loud, boisterous, often competing to be the biggest presence in the room. They seemed to all unconsciously mimic the voices of one another, for each of them spoke with the same colourless inflection and shouted in grinding, monotonous expressions. And they all had their hair in the same way, and on that special day when we could come dressed in our own clothes, I realised they all dressed in the same way too. In the changing room, I attempted to carve myself into their frigid normalities, so they could recognise me as one of their own species, or at least someone who contained a recognisable fragment of whatever it was they possessed. And it worked, until the day I painted stars and hearts and interconnected shapes of a myriad of colours on my hands and arms in the art room. One of them noticed and ridiculed it, until they all laughed, all six or seven of them. I never knew that colours and disordered shapes could engender such wild fits of amusement. I cried about that, but eventually I got over it. I had soon somehow taught myself to remember that event and think not of them, but of the small group that came to me in the hallway afterwards and told me that they loved the things I had painted. There is not a single blemish in the state of kindness. We had a substitute teacher during one winter term, Mrs Phuong. She was Vietnamese, and she often told us about her culture. I was captivated by that. One day after school I went into the music room to pick up some pieces of paper I had left. Through a thin rectangular window in the door, I saw Mrs Phuong in the piano room. She was sitting playing the upright piano, her posture sturdy and unswerving, her eyes closed, and her head and torso were gyrating, moved by the mechanical swings of some ethereal substance. Her fingers were little supernovas, exploding splinters of sound, each finger multiplying itself into many and bursting, leaping, hurtling, gliding, propelling. On and on she played, and when the song seemed to be closing and I'd hope it would live on it would suddenly burst into another transcendental segment. Each push of a finger had an equal purpose. Every second was beautiful, kinetic, an edgeless vision. And when she finished, she opened her eyes slowly, leant back and nodded. It reminded me of the clouds after a heavy rain, the way they fade and depart quietly, but with that same triumphant feeling on their fading faces, a tacit acknowledgement that the job is done. She looked at me. I think perhaps I hadn't yet left because I wanted her to know how touched I'd felt by her playing. She grinned and gestured for me to come in, and so I did, I entered and then stood by her. There must have been a hint of wetness in my eyes for she was looking at me with empathy. I told her I loved the way she played, and we talked a little about the song. She wrote the name down for me because I was sure I would forget it. *Suite No. 2 in C Major, Op. 17: II. Valse, Presto* by Rachmaninoff. She asked me if I played at all and, with timidity, I told her I did, but that I only knew some rudimentary chords. Then I sat on the stool beside her and together we played a slow improvisation. I played the highs, she played the lows. Afterwards, she asked what the berry-stained pieces of paper were that I had left on top of the piano. I told her it was a short story I had written over the lunch break. She gleamed and told me that she loved stories, and I took this as a hint that she was opening up an opportunity in case I wanted to read it to her. I wasn't sure how to respond at first for I had never read a story of mine to anyone, but when I took the pieces of paper in my hand, I somehow knew I was going to read it to her. Sadly, I lost the pieces of paper almost immediately after, so the story doesn't live in my memory with precise detail, but from what I can remember, it was about a young girl, a fearless one. She walks through a public garden. She walks slowly and purposefully, as though she's waiting for something, something to arrive and bring light to her day. She spots, under a fallen tree, beside a vast array of demolished vegetation, a batch of purple tulips with light tips that almost seem to have been dipped in the whitest paint, and beside them lies a fallen one, alone in its own patch of ruined grass. This tulip is different. It appears puny, odd-looking; it is damaged and torn and its petals seem to lack an upwards structure — they are slanted, and their texture is moist. The colour of each petal is greying with hues of some faded metallic rainbow, and the lines around the edges are nearly translucent. The structure of the stem seems to be withering, for it is curling in unpleasant spirals. And the tulip is moving, barely perceptibly. She notices this when she kneels to see its features up close. But the girl is fearless, and so she holds it in her hands. Its convulsing body is delicate, diaphanous, and a clear crystalline liquid bubbles and drips out from the pistil. The liquid is thick and contains a sheen that glitters with a distinct combination of faint colours. She takes this peculiar tulip back home and rests the broken thing on a velvet pillow where it continues to convulse and squirm. And then she hears it squeak, again and again, and it moves in tiny fits as though it's trying to tell her something. The squeaking appears broken and distorted but as she leans a little closer she begins to discern tiny words. She places her ear right up close to the tulip, creature, hybrid — at this point she is struggling to distinguish exactly what it is. Through a fractured squeak of a voice it tells her that it needs her help. The girl is shocked, speechless. She cannot believe a flower is talking. But she is young, and her wild imagination still blossoms, and so after a moment to catch her breath she asks the little creature how it can possibly talk and what kind of species it is exactly and then places her ear beside it. It tells her it is a special tulip. And then it tells her its name. I cannot remember what I had named it, but I know it was strange and multisyllabic and the letter began with A. So for the sake of realism, I'll make one up here: Arbosylo. Arbosylo struggles to speak, but manages to tell the girl that its frail body has been trampled on and greatly damaged, and it has only a sliver of life left. It tells her that she must take it up to a much greater height, as high as she can get. Arbosylo talks in broken words, and then it begins to lose all energy. It seems that it has become too strenuous for its mangled body to talk. In a worrisome cry, the girl tells Arbosylo that she'll try as best as she can. She takes it up to the top floor, right beneath the chimney crown. Arbosylo manages to push out the words "outside" and so she holds its moribund body outside the window. Arbosylo does not move, but instead pushes out a struggling word: "higher". The girl places Arbosylo in a little bucket and heads to the hill in a local park. She runs up the hill, stopping now and then to see if anything happens to Arbosylo. When she gets to the top she looks down at the poor tulip and takes it into her hands, noticing that it is now quivering with an ultra-fast vibration. Suddenly, Arbosylo lifts an inch from her hand, suspended in the air, before losing momentum and falling back onto her palm. It seems that even the hill is not high enough, and Arbosylo manages to utter the squeaking words "a little higher". The girl becomes distraught as she is unable to think of any place higher within her reach. She thinks as hard as she can. And no sooner does she begin to lose hope than a rising hot air balloon comes into sight. She watches the air balloon hover in the air, and soon it reaches a height greater than where she stands, and it goes up, and up, and up. With focussed speed, she makes her way down the hill and then gets on a bus towards the air balloon site. Arbosylo sits in the bucket, furrowed and torpid and losing vigour with every passing minute. The site is a wide field of grass, and all around are hot air balloons with pilots standing in the baskets heating the air inside. She runs up to one of them and begs to join, but the pilot looks at her brazenly and tells her to get going. She runs to another and does the same, and this time her voice is on the verge of breaking. There are three of them standing in the basket, and the pilot turns to her and tells her that they have reached the passenger capacity. Now on the brink of panic, she runs across the field and tries another. She begs the pilot with every fibre of urgency she can effuse. The pilot slowly takes off her hat and aviator goggles. She is old, very old, and her wide eyes glow and her smile is large and fanciful. She points to her ear and leans in closer, suggesting that she didn't quite catch the girl's words. Again, she begs the pilot, wiping tears from her eyes. The pilot halts and then looks at her with surprise and sincerity and then opens the basket door, patting her dearly on the back as she enters. The burners send heat rising through the envelope, and soon they take off, up and up, into the air. Arbosylo begins to move sporadically. They rise and they rise and the higher they go the wilder Arbosylo's body convulses and vibrates. Up higher they go and the girl hears Arbosylo squeaking again, so she holds it in her hand and up to her ear. Arbosylo is invigorated with life that seems to grow with the rising height. It squeaks into her ear and tells her that it owes its life to her and how thankful it is. It tells her that it has already broken a great rule by communicating with her, and that it is about to break another by telling her its real pursuit. Arbosylo tells her that it is not a tulip as it may seem, but it is in fact a star, disguised as a tulip, sent down to observe and examine up close the happenings of her world so it can bring that information back to the ether. The lower its body is on ground, Arbosylo tells her, the harder it is to garner the strength needed to ascend and rise back home, for where humans walk exists a field of energy that it must transcend to be able to return, and after the damage of so many wounds, it needs to be in a place that is as far away from as many humans as possible. But it can feel it happening, Arbosylo tells her, it can feel it summoning the power to leave. And at the highest height, in her open hand she lifts Arbosylo to the wandering clouds. The pilot watches and cheers hysterically. Arbosylo begins to shake and spin around and squeal with euphoria, and very quickly starts oscillating in the air above her hand, gliding across the lines of enigmatic shapes. And then, in a blinking instant, the girl watches Arbosylo rise and become sucked into the sky, quickly vanishing into nothing. Immediately after I had finished reading and placed the papers onto my lap I looked up to Mrs Phuong. I couldn't tell if she loved it or hated it for she exuded a look that was so acute but difficult to read; she kind of tilted her head, scrunched her nose just slightly and fixed her eyes on a space between us. But the next morning she surprised me in the hallway by approaching me and jubilantly telling me that she had been thinking of my story in the night, wondering if I'd like to read it to the class. I was a little red in the face at such a daunting request, but her liveliness emboldened me; something that lived in her enthusiasm, in the way she encouraged me, had seeped into me and enlarged the space through which I allowed my inner thoughts to travel. So I did. Mrs Phuong stood in the corner of the room. I occasionally looked up to her in little breaks to take a breath, and she was nodding and smiling at me profusely, softly shrinking the fidgety agitation summoned by my growing fear of so many invisible opinions. And somewhere in my mind I could hear the song she played, the way she let her world fall onto the keys, I could hear it beating between the curves of every sentence. Everyone in the room was listening, and as I read, in the back of my head I wondered about all the different worlds of this story and all the ways it was expanding and flourishing in those immeasurable minds sitting here before me. They were only words, characterised by simple trails of ink and combinations of letters, a linear structure that existed on paper in the same way from every angle. But it was through the mind that receives these words that they could paint the elements of any depiction, that they could be anything, truly anything. When I had reached the end I had forgotten where I was standing. I had even forgotten about the story. It didn't matter anymore. Now only silence pervaded the area, the silence of ideas settling into this enclosed space, and through the minds of disparate bodies. Silence leaves room for anything. Anything. And here amongst us was an air that could indeed take the form of anything. What small word would be the next to emerge? Who would speak it? How would we shift into the next phase of this instant? I don't remember what was going through my mind, perhaps not much at all, but in hindsight, I like to imagine myself thinking of this particular silence that lay between us, designed by all of us in the room. Our silence had escaped the normalities, our silence had embraced an ultimate diversity, and we had found, whether we had realised it then or not, in this area that had become ours, that real goodness cannot live from limited expectation, that to embrace diversity is to discover beauty. How incredible, I imagine myself thinking as I lower the pieces of paper and look up, it seems to me there truly are no gates through which our thoughts cannot pass, for the world we find ourselves in may be the same world from one all-encompassing perspective, but it in fact comes to be infinitely different shapes within us all. And even though we cannot truly feel what we have not lived, if we are to try to understand, if we are to try to get beyond the borders of what we already know, all we have to do is listen. All we have to do is let it in. That day I walked home with the wind beneath my feet. Passing by the park, I saw the shadow of a bird sail along the building beside me, soaring up and down and around, coming and going, coming and going. Then the bird emerged from the tree. It was a dove. A ringneck dove. It flew up and then dived down and landed on the tip of a fountain statue. I stopped to look at it, finding the stillness it had shown me. And then it looked at me, well, I like to think it was me the dove set its eyes on, and I like to think it was telling me something because I was endowed with a sense of happening, yes, of happening. We are meant to happen. We are happening. And then it flew away. And then I walked on, further, further into the day. And the day was good, and the day was closing, but soon, there would be another.

Printed in Great Britain
by Amazon

39076887R00067